Suspect

"Go inside and take your clothes off."
"Abruptly she laughed, 'What would you do if I refused—strip them off me yourself?' "
"You can make this as tough or as easy as you like, Linda. I'm not playing any more."

Federal Agent Reed Smith always did a thorough job when searching a suspect—even if it was a gorgeous blonde who didn't like the idea of taking off her clothes for strangers.

Smith knew that she was tied up with the dope racket in some way, but he didn't know the lengths to which she and other beautiful women would go to head him off the trail of one of the dirtiest and most dangerous games of his career. The mob he was after had power and influence, its tentacles reached into the highest places. Smuggling narcotics was big business for this gang—it would crush the life out of anyone who threatened its power. And Reed Smith was an even bigger threat than the corpses he discovered when he set out on his dangerous hunt.

Contraband

BY

CLEVE F. ADAMS

To Robert Leslie Bellem,
my favorite genius, and
to B.B., his favorite blonde

Fiction House Edition July 2022

isbn 978-1-64720-606-2

Fiction House Press
www.FictionHousePress.com

Chapter 1

Smith was earnestly explaining to the garage man a number of things that might be wrong with his car, and the mechanic was trying to convince Smith that there was nothing at all wrong with it. The man had all kinds of analyzers and high-powered gadgets to prove he was right, but Smith was stubborn. He kept insisting, and finally the mechanic decided there was no sense in chasing business out the front door and conceded that the car certainly was in bad shape. Smith told him to fix it. He was watching the girl with the Cadillac convertible and he had to have some sort of excuse to stick around.

It was a big garage, very high-class in every respect. There were at least a dozen mechanics on duty, and a floor manager and a cashier and nice red-leather-and-chromium chairs for the customers to wait in. Smith chose one of the largest of these and picked up a magazine. If it hadn't been for the gasoline fumes he'd have thought he was in a barber shop, everything was that clean and shiny. Rain drummed noisily on the overhead skylights.

The girl came over and planted herself smack-dab in front of Smith's chair. She was a very nice-looking number indeed. He placed her height at five-five; weight, around one fifteen; color of hair, L. brown; eyes D. brown; race, Caucasian. Visible scars, moles, or other distinguishing marks, none. Smith believed, however, he would have no trouble remembering her. She was quite lovely. Direct, too. "See here, are you following me?"

He feigned astonishment. "Do I look like the kind of man who would—"

"You look like the kind of wolf who would follow anything in skirts, but that isn't what I meant. Are you or are you not a detective?"

"Well," he said mildly, "that's a debatable point. Some say I am, some say not. I can't ever quite make up my mind."

She was furious. You could see that with half an eye. "I suppose my father hired you to spy on me!"

"I wouldn't know whether you even own a father," Smith said. He smiled at her, what he considered his most engaging smile. "I'll tell you this though. If you really have a father, he positively did not hire me. I'm not for hire."

"Then why are you following me?"

"Did I say I was, precious?"

She tapped a foot impatiently, studying him. Finally she turned on her heel and went over and spoke to the mechanic who was working on her car. He in turn went over and whispered to Smith's mechanic. They both examined Smith with hostile eyes. Then they came over and stood in front of him. One of them carried a wrench that must have weighed at least fourteen pounds. He hefted this suggestively. "Get out."

Smith was a long man, long and thin, and apparently he was afraid he'd break in two if he moved without great care. It took him quite a while to stand up. His lean dark face had a mildly sardonic look, like an amiable Mephisto's. He said in an aggrieved voice: "Well, if you don't want my business—"

The man with the wrench said, "You ain't got any business, bud. Unless maybe it's monkey business."

Smith looked at the other mechanic. "You find out what was wrong with my car?"

"There wasn't anything wrong."

"Oh well," Smith said, "some other time, then." He went over and carefully inserted his length into the car. The girl watched him with a mixture of triumph and disgust. He lifted his hat politely. "Tattletale." He then drove out of the garage and parked directly across the street.

When the Cadillac convertible presently nosed out into the rain and turned south on the San Diego-Tia Juana highway, Smith took up the chase where he had left off. He neither crept too close nor lagged too far behind. After a series of profitless maneuvers the Cadillac finally straightened out and ran like hell. Smith's car, seemingly without effort, stayed in the same relative position to his quarry. The windshield wipers smoothed rain from the glass in neat half circles. Visibility, excellent. Time, four thirty p.m.

Presently, less than a mile from the international border, the Cadillac braked recklessly to a skidding stop. Smith stopped too. The girl's car executed a roaring reverse, backing into the center lane until it flanked Smith's. The girl leaned over and rolled her right-hand window down. Her face was less than eighteen inches from Smith's. She was very, very angry. "I simply will not have you following me like this. I'll—I'll call a policeman!"

"That would be interesting," Smith said. He looked

pointedly up and down the deserted highway. "You'll have to call pretty loud."

She bit her lip. "My father did hire you, didn't he?"

"Not unless I've been drinking more than usual and forgotten it. Maybe if you'd tell me why you think your father should hire someone to watch you, I'd remember."

Two tears formed on her lower lashes, trembled there, broke off, and rolled down her cheeks. Smith reached out, touching one of them with a lean forefinger. "Real," he said in a detached voice. "I thought they might be glycerine. You know—like in the movies." He jerked his finger away as she bit at it.

"Oh, damn it," she said in a discouraged voice. And then, with returning spirit: "I hate you!"

"I don't hate you," he said. His mildly saturnine face became sad, as though he couldn't understand why anyone should dislike him. "I think you're lovely." He really did, too, but she was unappreciative. She slammed into second gear, ripped around in a wide U-turn. Her rear bumper took part of Smith's front fender with it. He turned more sedately. They went back to San Diego in the same approximate order in which they had left it. He watched her garage the Cadillac in the basement of the tall, exceedingly expensive apartment building. It was now slightly after five o'clock.

After a while a thickset man in baggy blue serge came out of the apartment lobby and crossed the street to Smith's side. "Anything?" His name was Cassidy and he was a pretty good drinking companion, though without Smith's capacity.

"No," Smith said. He didn't say anything else. The thickset man recrossed the street, shook rain off his hat, and disappeared inside the lobby. Smith took a paper-wrapped drugstore sandwich out of the dash compartment, unwrapped it, chewed at it with patent distaste. He deeply regretted the twenty cents he had paid for it.

At six o'clock he started his motor and rolled down to the corner, where presently he was joined by the thickset man in baggy serge. Cassidy stank of wet wool and cigar smoke and, more faintly, of Lucky Tiger, for he was deathly afraid of becoming bald.

"Frankly," Smith said, "you stink."

"That makes it unanimous," Cassidy said. "You and me both, only mine is strictly physical." When Smith refused to be drawn into an argument on the subject he lapsed into a sullen silence. They rode down to Civic Center and went into the post-office building, up to the second floor, through a series of offices into a large one, where they faced a third man across a broad mahogany desk.

This man was modeled in varying tones of gray. His close-cropped hair was gray, his eyes were gray, his suit was gray. He was the most colorless man Smith had ever seen. He was Smith's boss. He said, with a sort of grayish inflection: "Well?"

Smith was gloomily triumphant. "I told you it wouldn't work. She thinks I'm either on the make or a private dick hired by her father, who the hell ever he is. She damn near had me thrown out of a garage." He muffled a belch behind a lean brown hand. "These factory-made sandwiches will be the death of me yet."

The gray man smiled fleetingly, looked at the thickset man in baggy serge. "Well, Cassidy?"

Cassidy gnawed the end off an evil-looking cigar. "I prowled her apartment again. Still nothing there. She had a phone call just after Smith brought her back. I couldn't listen in without showing myself, but I checked it later. It was from Falconer."

The gray man came suddenly to life, slapping a flattened hand on his desk. "Of course it was from Falconer!" He drew a deep breath, went on more quietly. "Everything we've got points to Falconer. We know the girl used to be a frequent visitor at his place; we know she doesn't go there any more. That in itself looks suspicious. On the surface she is avoiding him, yet he contacts her by phone. She's made a round trip across the border every day for two weeks, but do the inspectors ever find anything? No. Yet the stuff continues to come in. Pounds of it." He broke off to stare fixedly at Smith's face. "Pardon me, am I boring you?"

"No," Smith said. He shook his head from side to side. "No indeed."

"Did Cassidy tell you who she is?"

"Cassidy never tells me anything," Smith said, adding sadly that nobody ever told him anything. He appeared to brighten a trifle. "That's what makes my success so remarkable."

"Hah!" the gray man sneered. He pointed a finger at Smith's nose. "She's Owen Van Owen's daughter, that's who she is!"

Smith was genuinely surprised. The Van Owen name was practically synonymous with San Diego County, what with all the oil wells, ranches, canneries, tuna-fishing fleets, and one thing and another. "All those millions?"

"That's what makes the case unique," the gray man said. "Though she isn't—or won't be—the first rich little girl that's gone wrong." He stared very hard at Cassidy, who was trying without much success to get the cigar lighted. "We still don't know why she's living in that apartment instead of the Van Owen mansion."

Smith moved his long body over to the windows, carefully, saying that he thought he might have ulcers. He stood looking out at the brightly colored lights of the city and harbor. The Coronado ferry, gaudy in rhinestone brilliants, crawled across black velvet water to the island.

Cassidy said fretfully: "It don't stand to reason for a gal like that to be kiting heroin across the border. It wouldn't even if we could catch her upholstered in the stuff."

"Have you anything better to suggest?" The gray man's query was tipped with acid.

Cassidy admitted that he hadn't. Smith, not turning from his inspection of the night, said the young lady was obviously afraid of something, all right. "She kept harping on that private-dick angle; believes it's her old man who's having her tailed." With his hand he smothered a mild eructation. "Why should she think that?"

"You got that dissipated look," Cassidy said. "You know, interestin'. All private eyes are dissipated and interestin'."

"I could press the acquaintanceship still further," Smith offered. "One could learn to be very fond of Miss Van Owen, even without the incentive of ninety-seven million dollars."

"It mightn't be a bad idea," the gray man said. "Neither the customs inspectors nor our people have turned up anything tangible in the usual manner. Perhaps you can scare her into something."

"If she knows anything," Smith said. He decided that his pessimism was due to hunger and the need for a bath. "You might fill me in on any minor details you think I should know."

"There's not much," the gray man confessed. "All we've really got on her is that she runs around with a fast crowd. She took a flier at George Falconer's games, quit that, and began bucking the tiger at Lupe's casino across the border. Nothing unusual there, especially for a girl with all that money behind her. Still—"

"Maybe they're shooting the stuff over the line with howitzers," Smith suggested. "Or model airplanes." After a while he took off his hat, looked in it, said: "Nuts!" and put the hat back on again. Presently he went out of the office, bending his head a little as he went through the door, though there was really no necessity for this. He had two whole inches of clearance.

Chapter 2

In this hotel room Smith bathed and shaved and chose a dark suit that was calculated to make him look less tall and slightly more "interesting," as Cassidy would have put it. Then, carrying his hat and the newer of his trench coats, he descended to the hotel grill, where he ate moderately well, consuming two bottles of ale with his steak. He then went out into the rain and hailed a cab.

It was 7.32½ by his wrist watch when he pressed the buzzer under the neatly engraved card of Miss Linda Van Owen. Down the hall, in a window embrasure, a man with a face like an inquisitive weasel's parted concealing drapes to examine him. Smith waved a casual hand. Harry Gee's weasel face vanished behind the drapes. Miss Linda Van Owen opened her door. She was dressed for the street, although, like Smith, she had changed. She appeared older than she had that afternoon, and a trifle on the haughty side, but she was still definitely lovely. She was not glad to see Smith.

He lifted his hat. "Did you know it was still raining outside?"

Two bright spots of color burned high up on her cheeks. Her D. brown eyes had angry golden flecks in them, like a cat's. "I told you I wouldn't have you following me. I meant it!" A small right hand went into a pocket of her mink coat and came out with a little silver-and-pearl gun. She pointed this in the general direction of Smith's belt buckle. His stomach muscles contracted unpleasantly. He had to be very careful of his stomach.

"Now, Linda darling," he protested, "is that nice? Here I am, trying to do you a favor, and you—"

"Get out!"

He sighed. "Oh, very well, if that's the way you feel about it." He turned away sadly, right hand pretending to struggle with his hat. His left hand, perfectly aware of what his right was doing, performed a sort of double-jointed maneuver and came around behind him and twisted the little gun out of her fingers. The gun was in his own topcoat pocket when again he faced her. "You ought to be ashamed of yourself."

She stamped her foot. "Listen, you tell my father—"

"I don't know your father," he said. "I have since found out that you have one, though." He smiled amiably. "Convenient things to have, fathers. They give you a certain standing in the community."

Her shoulders drooped rather pathetically. "Why must you persist in lying about it? It's perfectly obvious he's having you follow me." She stiffened again. "And let me tell you one thing: if he hopes to patch up our quarrel by such tactics as these, he can go find himself a lake to jump in!"

Smith nodded. "I like that, I do indeed. It shows the modern trend. Our parents, by God, are not going to run our lives for us, are they?"

She regarded him suspiciously. Then, as unpredictable as any of her sex, she backed off a step. "Come in."

"Thank you." He went in. Beyond the foyer was a comfortable living-room. It was not, perhaps, as heavily magnificent as any of the thirty-odd rooms in the Van Owen mansion at La Jolla, but it was nice. It was so much nicer than Smith's hotel room that he considered voting the Communist ticket at the next election.

She offered him a chair and he sat, placing his hat on his bony knees as though he didn't expect to stay very long. She let the mink coat slide from her shoulders, took a chair opposite him. It may or may not have been accident that one of her silken legs was exposed to almost the point where the silk ended. In any case it was a well-proportioned, not to say admirable leg, and Smith was properly appreciative.

"Now, then," she said, very business-like, "how much do you want?"

He appeared pleased at so practical an approach. "A fair question. The obvious reply is 'How much have you got?' "

"I knew it!" She was scornfully triumphant. "I've heard all about you private detectives. You take money from both sides."

"Of course."

She shrugged. "Well, I suppose it can't be helped. My father is hiring you to check on me and report. He would just love to find out that I haven't done such a good job of being independent, so he could tell me about it afterward. What have you told him so far?"

"Nothing," Smith said. "Nothing at all." He felt pleasantly virtuous at this one item of truth.

Her D. brown eyes probed his face. "I wish I could believe that."

"You can," he assured her earnestly. "Cross my heart, hope to die."

She continued to regard him for a moment, uncertain, patently distrustful. Then, arriving at a decision: "All right, here's what I want you to do. Go right on reporting to him, but don't tell him the truth. Let him think I'm doing fine. Don't tell him I've lost every dime of my own money and ten or twelve thousand dollars I haven't got."

Smith's face became waggishly cynical. "In that case I don't quite see how you expect to pay me for double-crossing him."

"But I'm winning again!"

"You are?"

"Yes." She took a breath and her eyes glowed. "In a week or so I'll have won enough to pay back all I owe and have something over for you."

Smith shook his head dubiously. "I don't like this contingent business. Haven't you any money now?"

"Just a little," she confessed. "I need that to go on playing. You see, I've been paying off this—this other debt a little at a time, because—well, because the party is becoming rather unpleasant."

"Falconer?"

She flushed. "So you know!"

"I've heard he could be unpleasant," Smith said. "Some say even nasty, but probably they're biased."

She nodded. "He threatened to go to Father and I couldn't have that, could I?"

"Of course not."

She gave him a brief, a sort of tentative, smile. "You know, you're rather a comforting person, even if you are a crook." When Smith didn't say anything to that, she went on enthusiastically. "I tell you, I can't lose! I've won every day I've gone across the border. I can't have you or anyone else stopping me now, can I? I mean, right when the end is in sight?"

"How is Señor Guadalupe standing up under this terrific beating you're giving his tables?"

Her eyes were starry. "Lupe isn't like Falconer. He's been positively sweet about the whole thing."

Smith stood up. "This I must see." He picked up her coat, held it outspread. "If money is that free in Mexico I might as well pick up a few dollars myself."

"You mean you're going over with me?"

"Why not? If I'm to take your proposition on a contingent basis I've a right to protect my interests, haven't I?"

She glared at him. "You're such a bastard. You're as bad as George Falconer."

"Not quite," Smith said. His face was a genial demon's. "I wouldn't trust you for twenty grand, even if I had it."

She looked at him from beneath suddenly lowered lashes. "Is money all you ever think of?"

"Now don't be coy," Smith counseled her. "Don't appeal to my baser instincts. Let's stick to money for a while." He leered down at her. "I like money."

"Yes," she said, "I'm beginning to realize that." Her golden eyes opened very wide and suddenly she laughed. "Well, you can't blame a gal for trying." As she slipped into the coat he held for her, the scent of her hair was in his nostrils, a little intoxicating, but his eyes remained cagy, calculating.

They went out of the apartment and rode the elevator down to the basement garage. An attendant in spotless white came out of a glassed-in cubicle, lifted his cap to Linda.

"You'll be wanting your car again, miss?"

"Please, Ralph."

Smith watched Ralph go away down the aisle between long double rows of parked cars. There was something about Ralph that he did not like particularly. The young man seemed a little cocky, a little too assured for an ordinary grease monkey. Not that one expected a garage attendant to be servile, but Smith had the uncomfortable feeling that this guy was laughing up his sleeve, probably at him, Reed Smith.

When the Cadillac convertible came rolling up the aisle and Ralph got out, Smith's resentment embraced the car too. Knowing how many times it had been searched, coming over the line, it was difficult to feel that it too wasn't laughing at him for a sucker.

"You'd better take it slow tonight, Miss Van Owen," Ralph said. "It's still raining." His mouth smiled at Smith. His eyes did not.

"Thank you, Ralph." She was composed now, quite the grand lady. She and Smith got in the car and they rolled out into the rain and turned toward the border. Neither said anything for several miles; not, in fact, till they were passing the exquisitely appointed garage where Smith had that afternoon been threatened with annihilation via a fourteen-pound Stillson. It was still open and apparently very busy.

Smith said casually: "What did they do to your car this afternoon?"

"Nothing."

"You mean there wasn't anything wrong with it?"

She half turned her head to look at him. "It was heating up a little, and the oil pressure showed only about fifteen pounds. I thought maybe there was a stoppage in the line. They didn't have time to find the trouble before your brazen effrontery made me so mad I didn't care if the darned thing blew up."

He made disparaging noises. "It seems to be all right now."

Another silence enveloped them, broken only by the rain and the sound of the motor and the hiss of the wipers. Then, as though genuinely curious, she said: "Were you always such a louse?"

"As far back as I can remember," he admitted, adding comfortably: "But you'll probably get used to me in time. You may even grow quite fond of me."

"God forbid!"

"I'm really a very likable fellow," he said persuasively. "You wouldn't consider even trying to think so?"

"No."

He subsided, watching the wet pavement unwind ahead of them, watching the raindrops dance in the beam of the headlights, watching her trimy shod foot on the accelerator. He was careful not to look too much at her profile because he was finding it increasingly difficult to keep his mind on his work.

Presently, coming to the barricade of the State Police and, beyond that, the customs sheds, he had a bad moment when one of the inspectors recognized him. This man, he felt, should be back driving a truck.

"Hello there, Smith!"

"Hello," Smith said.

The inspector recognized the car then, and the girl. He was embarrassed no end. Miss Van Owen looked at Smith with even less affection than usual. "So you know these lice too, do you?"

"Well, you know how it is. In my racket a guy gets around. You meet people here and there."

"Then maybe you can be of some use after all," she said tartly. "Maybe with all your influence you can keep them from tearing my car to bits when we come back." She glared as two other inspectors appeared like genii at her side. "You'd think I had a rumble seat full of Chinese or something. Or a gas tank full of jewels."

Smith let one eyelid droop slightly, the one nearest the dumb inspector. "You wouldn't accuse Miss Van Owen of smuggling, would you?"

"Certainly not," the man said. "Hah-hah." He looked at Miss Van Owen. "It's just a form, miss. We told you that."

He became painfully earnest. "We've got a new chief inspector that's hell on wheels. Honest, he'd suspect his own grandmother. Now, if it was me—"

Smith interrupted him. "Well, go a little easy on her, Meggs." He let his eyelid droop still further. "She's a friend of mine."

Meggs said he certainly would do this, yes indeed. He said that any friend of Mr. Smith's was and always would be a friend of his. They left his protestations hanging in mid-air and drove on across the border.

The Mexican officials' examination was so cursory as to be almost a farce. No one, their manner said, would be so stupid as to smuggle anything into Mexico, where everything was cheap and plentiful with the possible exception of American dollars.

A half mile or so farther on, the lights of Tia Juana glowed against the sky, multicolored and brilliant, giving the impression of a much bigger town. Abruptly the rain ceased, and a hesitant moon peeped out from behind scuddling clouds.

"Is your name really Smith?"

"Really and truly," he said. "Silly, isn't it?"

"Yes," she said. "Even you might have been more imaginative." Her slender foot pressed down hard on the accelerator pedal and they went through the town as though the fiends of hell were after them.

Chapter 3

The Mexican government's edict against gambling had, several years back, played havoc with the wealthier tourist trade, and especially with such million-dollar enterprises as Agua Caliente and El Mirador. Both of these luxury resorts had closed down tight, and when the new law looked as though it was going to stick they had been sold and resold a number of times, going rapidly to pot. But with the revival of horse-racing, even third-class horse-racing, it was thought in some quarters that the entire ban might eventually be lifted, and the man who called himself El Guadalupe had taken a chance on reopening El Mirador. The war and rationing in the United States had helped, luring a lot of people over the line who felt that large steaks, good rich butter, and plentiful liquor were irresistible. From that it was just a step for Lupe to take the gambling equipment out of mothballs and put it to work. Officially, gambling was still illegal, but either because of a local pay-off or because Lupe was a Mexican national rather than one of the American syndicates, he had been operating for some time now, and word-of-mouth advertising had brought him a nice, well-upholstered clientele. From the look of the parking area, the weather had done little to hurt business. There were forty or fifty cars, all sleek and shiny, nearly all with American license plates. A small wind rustled the myriad palms of the oasis, and in the main patio there was the heavy scent of rain-drenched flowers, the muted sound of dance music, originating somewhere inside the sprawling stucco-and-tile building.

Smith gallantly offered his arm to the young lady at his side, but it was ignored. She was seemingly in a very great hurry, her high heels tap-tapping ahead of him on the flagged walk. He decided that he had better take some thought of his own approach, since he was known here, although his profession was not. At least he hoped it was not. When presently he pushed through double-glass doors into a well-filled lobby, Miss Van Owen had already checked her furs and was on the point of entering the casino; then she ran into what appeared to be three very intimate friends. Two were men, opulent-looking men in dinner jackets Smith envied. He envied them even more the company of the lady. She was as vivid as a field of poinsettias at Christmas time, though in a refined sort of way. She was more glad to see Linda than Linda was to see her.

"Well, Linda!" she said, putting out both gloved hands.

"Hello, Eve," Linda said, and after the briefest of hesitations touched one of the gloves. Then with a cool nod for the men: "Hello, Chris. Hello, Father."

"What the hell," Smith thought. He was trying to make an unobtrusive exit when her voice halted him. "I'm sure you two must know each other. Mr. Smith, my father. Father, Mr. Smith." To the others she explained: "Mr. Smith is a sort of detective, you know." Her tone dripped malice.

"Smith?" Van Owen said. "Smith?" He was obviously puzzled, as he had every right to be. "I don't believe I know you, do I, sir?" He put out a large firm hand. "Not that I'm not very glad to, of course."

Perforce Smith shook the extended hand with a degree of enthusiasm. "One meets so many Smiths these days." Close up, he could see the reason Van Owen had accumulated all those millions. The elder man might have been fifty, possibly sixty, but there was no doubt of his vigor and personality. You felt that here was a man who knew his own mind and could tell others what was in it, but that he would always do it in as nice a way as possible. He was quite handsome.

After some little backing and filling—Linda, apparently, being the only one who didn't find the situation awkward—the other introductions were accomplished. The vivid lady, Eve, was Mrs. Dudleigh, and Chris Lancaster, pronounced Lankster, was her brother, though they looked nothing at all alike. Both had British accents, but not the affected, veddy veddy kind. To avoid staring too hard at the lady, Smith concentrated on Lancaster and found him a ruddy, healthy-looking specimen with nice teeth, smile-crinkles around his eyes, good hands, and a faint aura of excellent Scotch. He was thirtyish, and would probably sit a polo pony with complete aplomb. Brother and sister, it seemed, were almost next-door neighbors to the Van Owens in La Jolla. There was no reference made to a Mr. Dudleigh.

Smith excused himself and repaired to the checkroom, where he left his hat and trench coat. He discovered that the vivid lady and her brother and Owen Van Owen were right behind him, about to depart.

"Linda was joking, I presume," Van Owen said. "About your being a detective, I mean."

"Linda is quite a card," Smith agreed.

"Droll," Eve Dudleigh said, admiring Smith's length. "Detectives are supposed to be quite inconspicuous." Her eyes had the color of the sea at very great depth. They gave Smith goose pimples. He thought he would like to seize her and crush his mouth against hers, just to see what happened.

"Do you ride?" Lancaster asked. His voice was pleasant, friendly. His eyes were blue, serene, not green and exciting like his sister's.

"Ride?" Smith said. "Ride?" With some little difficulty he managed to remove his mind from Mrs. Dudleigh's mouth. "No, horses and I don't seem to get along at all." He wished he had a drink. "Not at all."

It was obvious that all three of them wanted to know more about this strange man they had found escorting their Linda, but they were polite. Van Owen contented himself with an invitation to lunch one day soon. "Where can I get in touch with you, Mr. Smith?"

Smith named his hotel. He had nothing to lose by this, for he was known there as a traveling auditor.

They said good-night again, and how happy they all were, and then he left them and went into the bar, where he drank two double ryes to sober up after the mental debauch he had just been on with Eve Dudleigh. Presently it occurred to him that he hadn't seen Linda for some little time; indeed, that she might have given him the slip, and he set about rectifying the matter.

He found her at one of the big double roulette layouts. There was a tremendous pile of chips in front of her, and her eyes were feverish. "A fine thing!" Smith reproved her. "I hope you're satisfied now."

She looked at him as though she'd never seen him before. "Satisfied? Oh, you mean about you and Father." Her smile was superior. "One would hardly expect you to come right out and admit it." She pushed a stack of chips onto the green numbers, scattered another stack indiscriminately over the board. Already she seemed to have forgotten him.

"You're sure you don't need a strong man to help you carry your winnings away?"

"I'll manage." She watched the croupier rake in her chips and everybody else's. "Why don't you go jinx some other table for a while?"

"God'll punish you for that," Smith said. He left her and went over to one of the less crowded crap tables, where he exchanged two twenties for silver dollars and began playing idly, never quite losing sight of Linda and her fluctuating fortunes at roulette. Music from the supper room floated into the casino, warming the emotionless drone of the croupiers, making pleasant and exhilarating the drab business of two or three hundred people trying to wring an illegal profit one from the other. Light from the great crystal chandeliers gleamed on women's bare shoulders, was absorbed by the sober clothes of men.

When the dice came around to Smith he surprised himself by making five straight passes, letting his winnings ride, not dragging down till he threw an eleven, which he felt was bound to be followed by craps. He was wrong about that, but he did seven out on a point of nine, so his judgment was more or less vindicated. Better than a hundred dollars to the good, he saw Linda leave the roulette wheel empty-handed and go toward the cashier's cage. Her face was so white that the make-up stood out like red ink on new plaster.

El Guadalupe came from the shelter of a cluster of palms and spoke to her quietly. Smith thought him beautiful. Except for the tiny waxed mustache adorning his too red mouth, Lupe might have been a plump and shapely woman. Anna Held never had more charming curves. A velvet dinner jacket molded these perfectly, and his jet-black curly hair was cut long over his ears and at the base of his neck. His eyes were liquid caresses. At something he said to her, Linda nodded in Smith's direction and he felt that they were talking about him. In this too he was presently proved right.

Linda had written and cashed a check and returned to her wheel, Smith had dropped his winnings and thirty of his original forty dollars when he felt a light touch on his arm. El Guadalupe smiled up at him. "May I speak with you a moment in my office, señor?"

"Why not?" Smith said. "I can't do any worse there than I'm doing here." Jingling the ten silver dollars in his hand he followed the smaller man to a door behind the cluster of palms and they went inside.

It was a slovenly office, considering the magnificence of the casino. The great carved desk had cigarette burns on it, and some of the cigarettes must have fallen off on the carpet, because that too had charred holes in it. Some of the upholstered chairs had been used as footstools, the boys not taking off their spurs first. Smith thought it was no wonder that El Guadalupe used perfume.

There was a man sitting over by the room's one window. He was very black for a Mexican and as slovenly as the office. Lank black hair straggled out from under his sombrero, and his sullen mouth was bestial. He was half-heartedly cleaning his fingernails with a throwing knife.

Lupe said: "Mr. Smith, this is my very good friend Solano." His voice was womanish, playful, but there was only a faint trace of Mexican accent. "Solano is my strength and sometimes my conscience. He is a great comfort to me."

"I can see where he would be," Smith admitted.

Solano said nothing at all. For just an instant his eyes lifted and met Smith's. They were gray striated with red and reflected the kind of hatred you associate with the eyes of a trapped animal.

Lupe sat down at the scarred, littered desk. "Just what is your business over here, Mr. Smith?"

"No business," Smith said. "I'm with Miss Van Owen."

"You claim to be a private detective?"

"I don't usually go around bragging about it."

Lupe's too red mouth smiled. "You are not listed in the telephone directory."

Smith riffled the silver dollars, stringing them out from one hand to the other. "I told you I didn't brag."

"And possibly you are not a private detective, yes?"

Smith allowed a normal amount of irritation to show. "Look, if you have anything important to say, say it and quit horsing around. I tire easily."

Without the slightest warning Solano threw the knife. It

missed Smith's ear by half an inch and whanged into the door behind him, where it stuck, vibrating like a tuning fork. "You will please to answer my master civilly," Solano said.

Smith's stomach muscles quivered in tune with the quivering knife. He was perfectly aware that the miss was intentional, that the half-breed's dexterity and control were admirable, but he did not like knives. He reached over his shoulder and yanked this out of the wood and carried it over to Solano balanced on the palm of one hand. "You are very good, señor," he said admiringly.

Solano reached for the knife, and Smith dropped it and drove a fist with crushing force against the bestial mouth. "You son of a bitch." He watched Solano and the chair go over backward. He discovered that he was sweating. He put his foot on the knife as Solano got to his hands and knees, then his haunches, wagging his great shaggy head from side to side. A trickle of blood and saliva oozed from a corner of the breed's mouth and he licked at it with his tongue. His eyes were almost all red now.

"Solano!" Lupe cried shrilly. "Stop it. You too, Señor Smith!"

From the tail of his eye Smith saw that El Guadalupe had a gun in his plump, womanish fist, and because the man who was so very like a woman in other things, there was no telling when the damned thing would go off. Smith retreated, careful not to make the slightest move that might be misconstrued. Solano stood up, righted the chair, sat in it, wiped his mouth on the back of his hand. Presently, tentatively, an eye on the man he acknowledged his master, he picked up the knife and thrust it into a scabbard at the back of his neck. He did not look at Smith.

A sound like repressed girlish laughter issued from Lupe's red mouth. "There now, that is better, no?" Watching Smith from beneath lowered lashes he rubbed the gun on the sleeve of his velvet jacket. "One hears rumors of a very tall man who works for your government, for the Treasury Department. Would you know of such a one, señor?"

"I don't think so," Smith said. He jingled his silver dollars noisily.

Lupe nodded as though this was the expected answer. "Then let us say that you are just an annoyance to my very dear friend Miss Van Owen. I suggest that the other side of the border is where you belong."

"All right," Smith said amiably. "I'll buy that." He turned toward the door leading back into the casino.

"Not that way," Lupe said. He tossed the gun to Solano,

went to a second door, and opened it. Cool night air came into the room, laden with the scent of flowers and rich wet loam. "This way, señor."

Smith looked at the unwinking eye of the gun in Solano's fist. "My coat and hat?"

"They will be sent to you."

Smith considered forcing the issue, but even if he didn't get himself shot, the best he could hope for was a bum's rush, since Lupe had plenty of other employees within call. He decided he would not make an international incident out of it. With Solano and the gun at his back he went through the indicated door. It closed behind them, and for a moment the night seemed pitch-black. Then he recognized the patio to his left, and straight ahead the parking area under the palms. He walked toward this, the half-breed's hulking shadow merging with his own. Solano's breathing was stertorous in the stillness.

Linda's car had been moved. It was in the same row but at some little distance from where they had left it. Even as he made the discovery, Smith knew that he wasn't intended to ride in the car anyway. Some slight change in Solano's breathing, perhaps a subtle shifting of the shadows at his feet, told him that the gun was being lifted and would presently club him down. He flirted the stack of silver dollars over his right forearm and into the breed's face. Then, loose-jointedly and without apparent hurry, he pivoted and kicked Solano in the groin. Agony doubled the man over. The gun fell from nerveless fingers and Smith scooped it up and brought it down smartly on the bowed head. He felt that besides the exigencies of the situation he had performed an act of mercy in thus blotting out the man's pain. Smith himself had once been kicked in the same vulnerable spot.

He discovered that there was cold sweat running down his ribs, and that his hand was shaking like an electric vibrator. Presently that stopped and he bent and hauled the senseless Solano into a clump of oleanders. The man's own belt and neckerchief and a strip of shirt served as bonds and a gag. Smith went over and got into the Cadillac convertible, screwing himself far down into the seat so that even his head would not be visible above the back. Solano's gun, beside him on the leather upholstery, was comforting. His face was peaceful.

As time went on, people came out and got in their cars and drove away. Other cars arrived, carrying people who were, on the whole, happier and more optimistic than the departing ones. There was a brief stirring among the oleanders, a muffled groan, then silence again.

It was fifteen or twenty minutes before Linda came out. Smith could not have told you how he knew that it was her high heels crunching the gravel, rather than another's, but he knew. She was alone. As she opened the left-hand door he straightened and smiled at her. "Hello, precious."

She did not scream. All she did was stifle a gasp against the back of a gloved hand. "They told me you'd gone!"

"People will tell you anything these days," he said, "but we can go into that some other time." He was no longer smiling. "Get in."

"I don't—"

He pointed Solano's gun at her. "Get in."

She was scornful of the gun. "If you've any idea of relieving me of my money, there isn't any."

Smith reached out and got a fistful of her fur coat. "The dialogue can wait till later, baby." He could hear Solano beginning to thrash about in the oleanders. "Coming?"

"All right." She slid under the wheel and started the motor. "Where to?"

"Home," Smith said, and put the gun away. After a mile or two, nearing the town, he said: I take it you didn't do so well tonight?"

Her profile looked white and strained. "No."

"Neither did I," Smith sighed. "Including the ten I threw in a guy's face I'm out forty bucks."

"You'll probably lie awake all night worrying about it."

"Not about the forty bucks," Smith said.

The lights of the town engulfed them, then there was another stretch of darkness until they came to the border. Traffic had thinned considerably and there was no line of waiting cars. Not even a halt was necessary on the Mexican side, but once across the international boundary they were immediately flagged down. Meggs and two other inspectors approached the car. Smith flipped the keys from the ignition and got out. "End of the line, Miss Van Owen." His face was that of a tired and disillusioned demon. He looked at the three men. "All right, take it apart."

"Not again!" Linda protested. "Not—" She stared incredulously at Smith's face. Then, cuttingly: "Oh, I see. You're one of them." She did not appear frightened. She was just a very angry young woman.

"Would you mind stepping out, miss?" Meggs asked. He had a curiously embarrassed air. "Make it easier all around, you know."

"Yes, I do mind." Her anger mounted to fury. "And you'd damn well better find something this time, or my father will—"

"Throw the weight of his millions around?" Smith suggested. He opened the car door, held it open. "Please."

She got out. "May I use the phone?"

"No."

For a moment her eyes hated him, Then, withdrawing from him a distance of perhaps six feet, she wrapped her coat about her and watched in grim silence as the men began wrecking her car. They took the hub caps off. They let all the air out of the tires. They probed and measured the gas tank, unbolted the muffler, and ran wires through the exhaust. Not finding anything in the harder places, they started on the luggage compartment and the car's interior. You could see that they had done all this before. They were expert. They could easily have got jobs on the assembly line with Cadillac. When it was all over they had not found anything in the way of contraband. They had not even found a marihuana cigarette.

Empty-handed and dirty and disheveled, they regarded Smith with active dislike. "And more good ideas?"

"One," Smith said. A step took him to Linda's side. "There's no matron on duty tonight, but there's a private room beyond the office. Go inside and take your clothes off. All of them. When you're through you can toss them out to me through the door."

Abruptly she laughed. "What would you do if I refused—strip them off of me yourself?"

"You can make this just as tough or as easy as you like, Linda. I'm not playing any more."

"I suppose not," she agreed. Some of the defiance went out of her shoulders. "Well, anything for a gag. Anything for Uncle Sam." She moved without haste toward the lighted customs shed. "Good old Sam."

He stood in the office until the door to the inner room opened a bare six inches and a slender naked foot pushed a pile of feminine clothes out at him. He put them on the counter and went through them methodically, inch by inch, panties, bra, everything up to and including the lush mink coat. He turned her handbag inside out and with eyes and fingers probed it and each item of its contents. He even tasted the powder in a jewel-studded compact. He found no evidence whatever of what he was looking for.

After a time he took a folded blanket from a cot by the wall and knocked on the closed door. When it opened a crack he thrust the blanket through. "Put this around you. I'm coming in."

There were no windows in the inside office, no cupboards, but he went over such furniture as there was with the same careful attention to detail. She stood huddled in a corner, watching him. "No one before has ever done to me what you have just done."

"If it will make you feel any better, I've never hated my job more." He did not look at her.

"Perhaps if you told me what you're trying so hard to find I could help you."

"Cocaine," Smith said, almost absently. "Heroin. The stuff that makes killers and prostitutes out of men and women. Sometimes children, if they have money enough to buy it."

She drew a deep breath. "And you could suspect me of that!"

"Certain things have pointed to you," he said. He finished with what he was doing. There was nothing. He got her clothes from the other room, brought them back, and laid them on a chair. "I'll ride into town with you when you're ready."

Chapter 4

Once more the broad highway unrolled before them, and as the distant glow in the sky which marked the city came nearer, the car became only one of many. With the cessation of rain the night had grown colder, and Smith, whose trench coat and hat were still on the wrong side of the border, was grateful for the warmth of the car. There was a sort of armed truce between him and his unwilling chauffeur, neither attempting even the barest civilities. Miss Van Owen seemed to be concentrating solely on her driving. Smith appeared to doze.

Then suddenly she said: "These certain things you imagine pointed to me—what are they?"

He saw no reason why he shouldn't tell her, now. The operation, this phase of it anyway, was finished for him. "Your connection with George Falconer, for one thing."

"But I explained that!"

"And very nicely, too," he said. "You haven't yet explained why, immediately after talking to you, El Guadalupe did his best to get me knocked off." He gave her a brief résumé of his encounter with the hulking Solano. "I'm assuming that Lupe just told you I had gone, not where I had gone."

She shivered, though not from the cold. It was growing warmer by the minute inside the car. "But I don't understand! If you're so sure of Falconer and the—the others, why don't you arrest them?"

"The man I work for likes to have proof when he goes into court," Smith said. "The unbeatable kind." He loosened his tie. "Why don't you turn the heaters off?"

"I haven't got— Oh, damn!" Abruptly she swerved into the outside lane and braked to a halt. "Look at that oil gauge: no pressure at all!"

"I feel better already," Smith said. "I was beginning to think I had a fever." Though he did not look it, he was quite alert now. Things seemed to be picking up again. He waited while she wrestled with indecision.

"That garage is only a mile or so farther on," she said finally. "The one where I stopped this afternoon. Do you suppose the engine will melt out from under us if—"

"I shouldn't think so," Smith said. He arranged himself even more comfortably. "Anyway, what do you care? Ninety million dollars will buy a lot of Cadillacs."

She slammed the car into gear, trod viciously on the throttle. "You're forgetting, aren't you? I make my living selling drugs to school kids."

"Now, now," Smith said. "Mustn't show temper."

They roared wide open down the highway and with a scarcely perceptible slackening of speed into the welcoming portals of the garage. It looked just as swank as ever, busy in a subdued sort of way. There was an entirely new crew of mechanics on duty. The floor manager was politely attentive to Linda, apparently not at all interested in Smith. After a time a mechanic was called into consultation, then a second. The car's hood was lifted and there ensued a considerable banging of wrenches and one thing and another. The consensus of opinion seemed to be that there was a stoppage in the oil cleaner. They sold Linda a new one. Neither of the men paid undue attention to Smith, nor so far as he could tell were there hidden meanings in anything that was said. They got a nice new oil cleaner from the stockroom, made the substitution and tossed the old cleaner into a refuse bin. The pressure gauge worked perfectly.

Linda paid something like six dollars for all this service, the men thanked her, she climbed in beside Smith and drove out into the night again.

"Wait a minute," Smith said. He reached over and removed the keys from the switch. The motor died.

"Good God!" Linda said. "Again?"

"I know," Smith said. "It's getting monotonous for me too." He got out, put the keys in his pocket, and went back inside the garage.

Every one of the mechanics was still in plain sight. Every one of them was apparently busy at an appointed chore. The discarded oil cleaner was exactly where it had been thrown, on top of a lot of empty cans and debris in the bin. One of the mechanics came over. "You forget something?"

Smith pointed at the filter. "That."

"You mean you want to take it with you?"

"I think so."

"But, mister, it ain't worth a dime!" He looked at Smith's face. "Well, of course, if you want it—" Shrugging, he found a newspaper and wrapped the thing up. "Okay, boss, it's all yours."

No one else in the garage evinced the slightest interest in the proceedings. Smith could not understand it. He took the bulky package, knew himself for an ass, and started to heave it back in the bin. Then, unwilling to admit this final defeat, he thrust the thing at the mechanic. "Look, take this apart, will you?"

"They don't come apart, Mister. They're sealed."

"Then use an axe, damn it!" Smith was immediately sorry for his tone. He apologized. He took a handful of change from his pocket and offered it as balm. "Go on, humor an old man with delusions. I want to see what's inside."

They went over to a workbench, where presently it turned out that the allegedly sealed container was not sealed after all. It came apart quite easily. And inside it there was none of the usual blackened and gummy filter material. Tight against one wall, a straight section of thin copper tubing led from one exterior connection to the other. The rest of the space was taken up by a nice shiny new can with about a pound and a half of heroin in it. This can, or others like it, had finally pinched the oil line shut.

"Well, I'm a son of a bitch," the mechanic said.

Hugging the can to him, Smith ran out the front door. Linda Van Owen and her Cadillac convertible had vanished.

For an instant Smith could not believe his eyes. Her keys were in his own pocket. Then he remembered a loose key he had seen in her handbag when searching it. Quietly but with great feeling he abandoned himself to such cursing as rarely came to his lips. The gray man was going to raise hell with him about this. He damned well should, too, Smith conceded. He went back into the garage and was directed to a telephone. As he gave the gray man's private number he was aware of a passing grease monkey who bent his knees and put his head far back, giving the impression that Smith was miles above him. "How's the weather up there?"

"I think there's a storm brewing," Smith said.

The gray man's voice came to him, faintly petulant: "Yes?"

"Well, not entirely," Smith said. "Sort of yes and no." He made no attempt to excuse himself, just stating the facts baldly and without embellishment. "I've got some of the stuff. I've got at least two witnesses here to prove where it came from. I don't know where the girl thinks she's going. She may even go back to her apartment."

"How about the garage people?"

"If they were in it they'd have done something about me before this."

"All right," the gray man said. He did not burn Smith's ear off with recriminations. He just said that quiet "All right," and left the rest to Smith's imagination.

Hanging up, Smith went down the row of cars and got the two mechanics who had exchanged a six-dollar oil cleaner for fifteen or twenty thousand dollars' worth of heroin. He persuaded them to solder the can tight and scratch their signatures on it for purposes of identification later. They and the floor manager also signed a make-shift affidavit. The other mechanics all stopped their work to stare at Smith with a mixture of awe and incredulity. One of them voiced an apparently common thought.

"For a dick he's about as inconspicuous as the Eiffel Tower."

"Well, that's the goddam government for you."

Smith's mind was still wrestling with such phenomena as Linda's flight and the careless disposal of a sizable fortune in an open refuse bin. As he had told the gray man, it was obvious the garage people weren't part of the ring. Otherwise he, Reed Smith, would not be standing here unmolested. Then why had Linda picked that particular spot to dump her hot cargo? As a matter of fact, she needn't have dumped it at all. She could very well have limped into town in spite of the car's overheating. Was it possible that she herself didn't know about the fake cleaner and its contents? This was a charitable and even pleasant thought, but he had to abandon it because in that case there was no sense to her running out on him. A rather ridiculous idea occurred to him and he asked who had the contract to pick up the empty cans and stuff from the bins.

"Acme Refuse. They come around once a week, Saturdays."

This was Tuesday. Smith thought it most unlikely that anybody in his right mind would leave twenty grand lying around for that long a time. Maybe Linda didn't care about the twenty grand. Maybe she thought her pretty neck worth more than that. On the other hand, she may have seized her moment's freedom from surveillance for no other purpose than to summon reinforcements, who even now might be on their way out here to retrieve the loot.

On the off chance that this was possible he decided to put his prize in the garage safe and stick around for a while. A half hour went by and he had seen no carload of hoodlums equipped with tommy guns. He hadn't even seen a small boy with a water pistol. He began to feel a trifle silly, sitting there with a gun in his own fist while the garage manager took care of such routine chores as running up a batch of invoices on the adding machine.

The telephone rang. The manager answered it, passed it across the desk. "For you."

"You'd better get in here," the gray man said. His voice was remote emotionless. "We're at Miss Van Owen's apartment. Gee has been shot."

Harry Gee was the weasel-faced man who had been stationed in the hall outside Linda's front door. Smith licked suddenly parched lips. "Dead?"

"Yes."

Smith tried to keep his voice as emotionless as the Old Man's. "The girl?"

"I'm afraid so," the gray man said. "We'll ask her about it—when we find her."

Chapter 5

The street outside the Carondelet Apartments was not deserted, but there was no crowd such as usually springs from nowhere immediately before or after the arrival of the cops. A prowl car with two uniformed men in it was nosed into the curb, its radio muttering, but the men weren't doing anything, just sitting there. In the Carondelet there were quite a few windows alight, and up and down the block there were more, but on the whole you would say that sc far the business had been handled with discretion. A second police car, this one a plain black sedan, was parked a few doors down. No one was in it. In the entrance to the basement garage ramp the attendant, Ralph, apparently up for a cigarette and a breath of fresh air, nodded to Smith, took a last drag on the cigarette and snapped the butt at the gutter. He looked clean and neat and bored.

Inside the lobby Cassidy was talking to a worried man in pajamas, robe, and slippers, who turned out to be the Carondelet's manager. Along the lower hall there were a few open doors, and a small knot of tenants in varying stages of undress hovered near by. Cassidy advised the manager to tell the tenants they might as well go to bed, there was nothing to see, really, just a dead man, and even he wouldn't be available for viewing purposes. Cassidy was pretending that the passing of one Harry Gee had not affected him at all; it was just another one of those things, like finding your car with a flat tire when you're all dressed up and late for the party. As a matter of fact, he was all dressed up. He had abandoned his baggy blue serge for a sharp new gray gabardine. There were freckles the size of peas on the backs of his hands. "Well, it took you long enough," he said.

"My hacker was a stranger in town."

They rode the automatic elevator up to the fourth floor, where a third uniformed cop was telling some more half-dressed tenants that they ought to go to bed, there was nothing to see, but in case something interesting turned up he would let them know, personally. Smith recognized him as Captain Dietrich's driver.

It was Dietrich himself who let them into the apartment. Hard cold eyes looked Smith up and down, and his thin-lipped mouth twisted as though he had bitten into something unpleasant. "Oh, it's you. What else have you managed to bitch up?"

"We can't all be detective captains," Smith said mildly, and went past him into the living-room. He saw with some surprise that Linda's father was there, talking quietly to the gray man. He saw too that someone had thoughtfully spread a white shag rug over the body of Harry Gee. It looked like something a florist might have concocted for a child's grave. There was a faint fragrance in the air, reminding him of Linda, had he needed reminding.

"I think you've met Mr. Van Owen," the gray man said.

"Yes."

They shook hands, and then for a moment there seemed nothing at all to say. Smith still found the older man's appearance, his manner, admirable, and if he was not exactly cheerful, that was to be expected. Even with ninety-seven million dollars to fall back on, a man might miss his daughter, especially if she were hanged by the neck until dead. As dead as, say, Harry Gee over there.

The gray man briefly sketched in recent developments, in so far as he knew them. On hearing from Smith he had got hold of the available men and sent them to such spots as it seemed likely Linda might head for. He did not name the spots, almost too studiously avoiding naming them, so that Smith knew Falconer was not to be mentioned. He did not know whether this was on Van Owen's account or Dietrich's, but guessed the latter. So far as was known, Dietrich's business was strictly homicide and he let other departments alone, expecting them to do the same for him. But he must have been aware that Falconer was running wide open within the city limits, and that some of his brother officers found it profitable to let him do so.

"We didn't really expect her to come back here," the gray man said. "But we did think we might find something of interest in the apartment. Just in passing, we looked in the garage downstairs and found her car was in." He sighed. "So we came up and found Harry." He lit one of his thin, dappled cigars. "Mr. Van Owen telephoned shortly after that, so I asked him to come up."

Dietrich said angrily: "And I'm still not sure she didn't call him first—to tell him she was in a jam." He thrust an angular, truculent jaw at Van Owen. "Maybe you can get my job for that, maybe you can't, but as long as I'm on it I'll work at it as I see fit."

Smith had the distinct impression that there had been some unpleasantness before this. Dietrich was not noted for tact and he hated a case in which Federal agencies were involved. Over by the front windows Cassidy made a vulgar sound with his mouth. "Go on and work at it. The Old Man called you, didn't he?"

Van Owen said politely that he had no intention of getting Dietrich's or anybody else's job. He sat down beside the gray man, borrowed a match, and lit a cigar of his own. Together they made an impressive pair: Big Business and its Confidential Secretary.

Smith was playing a little tune with a forefinger and his lower lip, like a faucet dripping in the bathtub. "I can't understand Harry jumping her in here. He had no reason to, unless—" He looked at the gray man. "He couldn't have known what happened way the hell and gone the other side of town."

"By God!" Cassidy said. "Now there's a fact, he couldn't have."

The gray man conceded that there was a point here, a small one, adding that there were a number of others that badly needed explaining.

"I know," Smith said. "She ran out on me, indicating that she knew what I'd find when I went back into that garage. But if she knew that, why come back here?"

Dietrich cursed. "Listen, this may all be very interesting and educational, but I'm a little sick of culture. I've got a body getting cold and the coroner's going to raise holy hell about it." His mouth twisted into a sneer for Smith. "Stop me if I'm wrong. This *is* her apartment, isn't it? She *was* smuggling happy dust, wasn't she? And Gee was on her, wasn't he?" He threw up his hands. "My God, she came back here because there was something here she wanted, or something incriminating to her."

"She was already incriminated."

Van Owen seemed to find something vaguely encouraging in this discussion. "Are you suggesting that perhaps my daughter didn't—" His eyes went quickly to the shag rug and what lay under it.

"I don't know what I'm suggesting," Smith said irritably. "I just know there's something here that smells." He looked at Dietrich. "Why didn't she take her own car?"

"Because she knew she wouldn't get far with it. It's hotter than a firecracker."

"There's that," Smith agreed. "For the same reason you'd wonder why she'd drive it all the way back here just to tidy up a bit." His brows drew down, accentuating his somewhat startling likeness to Mephisto. "I suppose you've buzzed the neighbors. Anybody hear the shot?"

Dietrich shook his head. "You'd hardly expect that. It's one o'clock in the morning."

"You look at him?"

"Enough to know he wasn't going anywhere he could walk."

"Mind if I do?"

"Help yourself. Don't move him."

The phone rang. For an instant no one stirred, looking at it. Then Cassidy picked it up, nodded to Dietrich. They all watched his face as though it might tell them something his words didn't. He hung up, worked some saliva into his mouth, spat at the fireplace. "Thought we had something.

Cab-driver with a frail from this neighborhood." He laughed. "Wrong frail, and I do mean wrong. She works out of a joint on B Street."

Van Owen winced. The thin panatela in the gray man's mouth moved up and down, disparaging the remark. Nobody said anything.

Smith went over and peeled back the shag rug, folding it neatly down, exactly halfway, his right hand patting the lower part gently, twice. His face gave no sign that he felt, or had ever felt, either one way or the other about Harry Gee.

The bullet hole was in Gee's lower left breast, a contact wound, the wool fabric scorched for a considerable area around it, where blood hadn't obscured the fact. The blood itself had long since stopped welling, but there was evidence that it had run in two directions, one rivulet apparently ignoring the law of gravity. Besides the blotting action of the coat fabric, something else seemed to have been laid over the blood, pressing onto it, and there were a few very short bristles that might have been hair, but could easily be jute from, say, a burlap bag. Smith looked at Cassidy and the gray man. "You didn't— He was exactly like this when you found him?"

They nodded, yes. Cassidy said: "The important thing at the time seemed to be the girl, not Gee. There was nothing we could do about him."

"Yes." Smith thought that a very frightened Linda might have attempted to stop the bleeding, but hardly with the weight indicated, nor with a material anything like a burlap sack. He stood up, and now his face looked lined, tired. "I don't think he was shot here. I think he was carried here, and in that case she didn't shoot him. It's a plant."

Dietrich was not dumb. He was, in fact, a very smart cop, but like the others he had not spent what seemed like precious time on minute details. On his knees beside the body he opened a penknife, picked one of the short fibers loose, nodded at Smith. "I can see a jute sack, maybe folded, with him lying on it over somebody's shoulder."

"Yes."

Dietrich got to his feet, snapped the knife shut. "You had something like this in mind awhile ago. I think I ought to know why." His manner was no longer truculent.

"Her coming back here bothered me," Smith said. "Like the thought that she might have run out on me for no logical reason—just a woman's reason. From her point of view she'd been picked on, humiliated, and accused of something pretty nasty. She saw a chance to pay me back for part of that and took it, that's all."

Van Owen cleared his throat. "You seem to know a great deal about my daughter, Mr. Smith."

"I spent some time with her."

Color came into Van Owen's face. "Meaning that I haven't spent enough?"

"Good God," Cassidy said, "let's not start that again."

"I'd like to go down and look at her car," Smith said. "It may confirm some of this. She either knew what she was carrying or she didn't. If she didn't, the rest of it makes sense." His eyes interrogated the gray man briefly. He was satisfied that Falconer's place was under observation; satisfied too that no attempt had been made to raid the highway garage for an oil filter that was no longer there. The garage people would have called.

They all went downstairs, and, seeing them, the youth Ralph came out of his little glassed-in cubicle. "Something I can do?" He followed Smith and Dietrich down the line of cars to the Cadillac convertible. Van Owen and the gray man and Cassidy watched from a little distance. Smith lifted the hood, bent to peer in at the motor. "Anybody else been interested in this, Ralph?"

"Two of the gentleman with you came in and inquired."

"That all?"

"Yes, sir."

Smith's eyes and his hands were busy with the filter. There was fresh oil around the connections, the metal of the top showed bright scratches. "Let's see, now, you'd have been standing about like this when he walked in on you." He straightened. "Right?"

Ralph's eyes were wide, his mouth half-open in surprise. "I, sir? Who? I don't get it."

"Sure you do." Smith looked around for something to wipe his hands on, finally used his handkerchief. "Somebody's been monkeying with this filter and not finding what he expected. You just said nobody else had been in. That kind of puts it up to you, son."

The youth's face grew pale with rage. "Listen, you bastards, you think you're gonna stick me for this job you're crazy. I don't know what you're talking about."

"Look, kid," Smith said patiently, "you haven't been anywhere. By the time you'd done what you had to do, my friends had been in and then the building was lousy with cops. If you'd lammed before, leaving him down here, you'd not only have the cops after you; your own playmates would think you'd grabbed the stuff. You were in a spot, all right." He took out his gun. "But it's over now. We'll find the sack you used, and the gun, and maybe one of your smocks with a little blood on it—"

Ralph took a backward step, looked from Smith to Dietrich. "All right, I guess I got nothing to lose by talking." He drew a deep breath, held it. Then he did a most surprising thing. With his hands out like a mammy-singer's he sank to his knees. "Jesus, mister—" He plunged head-first between Smith's legs, slid under the car like an eel, came up shooting from three cars down the line. His laughter was hysterical, maniacal. "Gonna find my gun! Why, come on, you bastards, here's my gun and see how you like it!"

A slug hit metal, glanced off it screaming, and burned Smith's neck. He dropped to the floor, crawled on hands and knees to peer around the car's rear wheel. Dietrich's gun spoke once, then again. Smith yelled at him: "Take it easy, he can't get out!" Up toward the front somebody else was exchanging shots with the kid now. Smith stood up, saw Cassidy scramble toward the space between two sedans; saw Ralph pop up from behind them; saw Dietrich, standing spread-legged in the aisle, take careful aim and fire. The kid went down, rolled into the open, stood up and ran crookedly, lopsidedly toward the street ramp. Dietrich fired twice more before Smith could get to him, prison his arms from behind. "For Christ's sake, cut it!"

Two uniformed cops came down the ramp, first their legs appearing, then their bodies, guns, heads. The youth Ralph raised himself on an elbow, pushed his gun out ahead of him. Police pistols made a sieve of him. Dietrich ran forward, drunk with triumph. "Kill a cop, will he? The son of a bitch won't kill any more!"

Smith leaned against the fender of somebody's Lincoln and was sick.

After a time he straightened and saw Cassidy standing there watching him. He wiped his mouth, his face on a handkerchief that was sticky, smelling of oil and grease. Distantly, faintly, he heard the gray man's voice as close to anger as it ever came: "Shouldn't be allowed—play with—firearms."

"I suppose it's no good asking," he said.

Cassidy shook his head. "Not after that." He brightened a trifle. "They've sent some guys over to where he lives—lived. They may find something."

"Sure," Smith said. "Falconer's life story, in Braille."

"Don't let it get you, bud. We haven't done so bad. We'll do better."

Smith looked at him curiously. "You wouldn't be like Dietrich, would you—happy because we knocked off a cop-killer?"

"I'd rather done it with my hands," Cassidy said. He stared down at them, shivered. "What the hell?" He discovered a three-inch triangular tear in the trousers of his new gray gabardine. "So help me Christ, I'm never going to wear a decent suit again!"

They found Linda in the back of a plushy Packard station wagon. Under a tarpaulin carefully arranged to look careless, she was a fur-wrapped mummy, the kid having used her own coat as a strait-jacket. Her crossed arms were roped at the wrists, the rope carried around in back and then downward to cinch her legs. Above a gag made out of cotton waste and adhesive gauze her eyes were wide, frightened. But when she recognized Smith the fright went away and she lay quiescent while they undid her.

"My God, am I glad to see you!" She picked surplus lint from her mouth. "Bloody as you are."

"Bloody?" He put up a hand to where the base of his neck seemed suddenly afire. He stared incredulously at what the hand brought away. "In the neck? A Smith?"

The knot of men up front was breaking up. Cassidy said quickly: "You got any questions, you better ask 'em now."

Smith nodded. "Did Ralph happen to mention anyone by name—Falconer, perhaps?"

"No, I—" She half-closed her eyes, trying to remember. "He was furious when he came up, and frightened too, I think. He wanted to know what I had done with the—the dust, he called it, and accused me of tipping off that so-and-so nasty-word dick, who wouldn't do any more snooping, by God, and neither would I." She drew a breath, blew it out through pursed lips. "So the party got a little rough, and I'm afraid that's all I can tell you." She felt of her throat, winced, and Smith saw angry bruises. "Except how glad I am to see you. I never thought I'd admit it, but I am."

Watching her, Smith knew she was perfectly aware of her father in the approaching group, but she did not turn until Van Owen spoke. "Well, Linda?"

"Oh, hello, Father." They might have casually met on the street, or in one of the broad halls of their own house. Then she said: "No, this is no time for repression," and went into his arms.

Chapter 6

There was a lady sitting in his room. He had been thinking about her off and on since their first meeting, and it occurred to him now that she was not there at all; that she was a figment of his imagination, a vision, albeit an altogether lovely and exciting vision, conjured up by a fevered and lecherous mind. Then he saw that she was quite real, that she was smoking one of his cigarettes and had somehow located his secret cache of liquor. She was Eve Dudleigh.

"I've been waiting for you a long time," she said. Her voice held mild reproof.

Smith closed the door behind him, leaned his back against it. "Aren't you afraid of being compromised? What will Mr. Dudleigh think?"

"He needn't bother you. He is, I hope, safely in hell by this time." She inhaled, blew a perfect smoke ring, something that Smith himself had never been able to do. He admired her elaborately.

"Is that any way to talk about one's husband?"

"About my husband it is."

Her faint British accent was enchanting. It provided an extra fillip to the rich warmth of her tone, the calm challenge in her sea-green eyes. It had the effect of making her a new kind of woman, a totally different kind of woman. In spite of considerable reading and hearsay evidence to the contrary, Smith still visualized the British female as cold and distant. Obviously this one was nothing of the sort, yet he remained slightly suspicious, as one will when confronted with an unaccustomed drink, like absinthe, say, which hints of forbidden things.

He came in and sat cautiously, tentatively, next her on the davenport and poured himself a drink. "You don't mind?"

"It's your whisky, darling."

"I know." He looked at the half-filled ashtray, noting with a kind of pleased surprise that her lipstick had not come off on the cigarettes. He looked at her mouth, and from that to her eyes. He had the curious sensation that they grew larger and that he could, if he wanted to, dive right into them and get lost. With something of an effort he returned his attention to the glass in his hand. "The clerk downstairs didn't think it was funny, your waiting to come up and visit me like this?"

She shook her head. "He suggested it." She laughed, giving Smith a new set of goose pimples. "This is not a very good hotel. He was afraid I was being annoyed."

"But you weren't?"

"Men never annoy me. I like them, even the more obvious kind."

Smith wondered if he was one of these. He said: "Then I needn't apologize for my hotel." He smiled at her. "I discovered that I could have much better quarters in a second-class hotel than I could afford in a first-class." He thought he had better get the financial phase over with at once. "I'm just one of the proletariat, you know."

She dismissed that with a wave of the hand. An emerald and diamond dinner ring on one finger had probably cost more than Smith's annual salary. "Tell me, are you really a detective?"

"Oh yes," he said. He drained his glass rather hurriedly. "Yes indeed."

"I thought at first that Linda might be joking. Then I—" She turned her glowing eyes full on him. In them, and on her luscious red mouth, there was amusement and a faint disdain. "Did you find anything interesting among my things?"

Smith was genuinely astonished. "Among your—" He put his glass down, carefully, as though it were very precious and fragile. Then, also carefully, lest he startle her into sudden violence, he managed to widen the distance between his knees and hers. "What the hell," he thought, "what the hell?"

She regarded him, still with that lazy amusement tinged with scorn. "Don't be frightened. I've no intention of going to the police. If I had, I'd have gone before this."

"I'm sure you would." He nodded, as though resolving an argument within himself. "Of course you would." He moved closer to her again and as though by accident let his hand rest on hers where it lay along her silken thigh. She was still wearing the same gown, a bodice of black drawn in tightly at the waist and then flaring excitingly into shimmering flame. "And I'm not in the least frightened. Just—puzzled." When she did not withdraw her hand, his fingers moved along it lightly, caressing it. "So I'm a detective, and I'm supposed to have searched your apartment or house or whatever. Is that it?"

"That's the essence of it, yes."

Her skin was cool to the touch, not cold but with an inviting coolness. "And what did I steal, if any?"

She shook her head. "Nothing was taken. That's why I knew it must be you—or Linda."

She certainly had a gift for prodding a conversation along. This was the third nudge in approximately five minutes. "Linda?" he said blankly. Then he said: "Oh, I see." He remembered that on that first meeting Linda had been considerably less enthusiastic than the others. He was now presumed to be in Linda's employ, whereas Linda herself had believed him retained by her father for an entirely different purpose. Considering that he was employed by no one but Uncle Sam, it was all very confusing. But not dull. No indeed, not dull. He gave his companion his complete attention. "Have you mentioned these not very charitable thoughts to Linda?"

"Would I?"

"I don't know," he said. He tried to see his own reflection in her eyes. "You seem capable of almost anything." He leaned still closer. "Would you mind very much if I—"

"Kissed me? Not at all. But if you want me to kiss you—" The green eyes darkened, became impenetrable. "That's quite another matter isn't it?"

"Well, just a sample, then." He kissed her. Her lips were full, warm, slightly parted, but there was no answering pressure. He felt that he had made progress, though. He saw that she was watching him, again with that faintly scornful expression.

"Why do men always close their eyes when they kiss?"

"You mean you didn't?"

"Of course not."

He saw completely new vistas opening ahead of him, like the first time he had tried opium. He felt that here was a teacher of merit, one who had sound if somewhat revolutionary ideas. He felt a new admiration for the British Empire. He wondered if her husband had died of natural causes. "May I offer you another drink, madame?"

"A small one, please."

After a time he said: "You know, I really think you should go to the police. The guy might decide to try it again. He might even attack you."

She was not worried about that either. It appeared that what did worry her was Linda. "I'm afraid that I'm partially, perhaps wholly, responsible for the rift between her and her father. I wish you could convey to her that I'm not—that he isn't—" She broke off to stare at him with eyes no longer amused and mocking. "Were you ever lonely?"

Smith admitted that he was, frequently. He said that in

fact he was lonely now, and she could help him if she would, but he saw that he was making no impression whatever. Her mind was still on Linda and Linda's father. "It's quite natural, I suppose, a daughter's jealousy under the circumstances, but that she should resort to spying, to—how do you put it?—to get something on me—" She drew a deep breath. "Well, I confess to being a little angry."

Smith was indignant. "If I didn't have such a sweet character I might be a little angry myself. Who walked in here and out of a clear sky accused me of pawing through your undies? You ought to be ashamed." He became earnest. He seized both her hands to show her how earnest he was. "Listen, I didn't prowl your house, flat, or apartment. I don't even know where you live. And it certainly wasn't Linda. I was with her practically all afternoon and evening."

"Then—?"

He nodded emphatically. "By all means report it to the police." He saw that she was convinced, or almost. "As for the rift, the last time I saw Linda she was in papa's arms. Maybe you'll be a stepmother yet."

Abruptly she released her hands, stood up. "Thank you, no."

"Not even for ninety-seven million dollars?"

She was drawing on her gloves now. "I suppose I deserve that. I let you kiss me, didn't I?"

"But for a good cause," he pointed out.

She shook her head, no. "I wouldn't have to seduce you to tell whether you were lying. For a time I thought we might be kindred spirits, that's all. I was mistaken."

He saw that she was really going to leave. Sighing, he got to his feet and held her cloak for her. "You're sure you were mistaken?"

"Yes."

With his hands on her shoulders he turned her about. He put his arms around her, bent her far back, and crushed his mouth against hers. This time he did not close his eyes. "Are you still sure?"

She released herself, not violently, but with surprising strength. She was breathing only a little faster than usual. "I don't know. I'll think about it."

"I'll think about you too," he promised with utter sincerity. His own respiration sounded a trifle ragged. "You wouldn't care to stay and do your thinking here?"

"No."

"Not even till I can get you a cab?"

"I have my own car, thank you."

"Then let me see you downstairs," he persisted. "Just to show you I'm really a gentleman at heart."

She nodded acquiescence to that. "Perhaps it's just as well that the staff sees you in good health when I leave."

He was still turning this over in his mind when they reached the lobby and went out to her car. He did not know whether she had reference to the devastating quality of her physical attractions or if she had unconsciously betrayed a knowledge of another man who definitely had not been left in good health; a weasel-faced man named Harry Gee, for instance. He thought this last most unlikely, but there was something, perhaps the cold night air on his bared head, that momentarily cooled his ardor. He pushed the thought from him and leaned in through the open window, but she would not let him kiss her again. "All right for you," he said.

"Good night."

Then she was gone.

As he turned to re-enter the lobby he was confronted by two men, bulky in overcoats, each with one hand bulky in an overcoat pocket. From some personal experience and seeing lots of movies he knew at once that the hands weren't in the pockets just to keep from freezing. The larger of the two men said gruffly: "Your name Smith?"

He considered denying it. He considered screaming for help, too, but it seemed improbable that any could get there in time to do him much good. It was two thirty in the morning, and except for three or four cars, one a limousine with its motor still running and presumably that in which the two men had arrived, the block was deserted. Behind the men the lobby was dimly lit and at the moment devoid of occupants other than a sleeping bellhop. Even the clerk was out of sight. Smith admitted his identity.

"We was just bein' polite anyway," the shorter man said. He was shorter, but he looked equally sturdy and durable. "We knew who you was all the time." He jerked his head at the limousine. The hand in his pocket jerked slightly in the same direction, as though head and hand were connected by a taut string. "The boss wantsa see you a minute."

"The boss?"

"You know, George."

"Oh, George!" Smith wondered why the hell a man as intelligent as Falconer should be resorting to an overt act like this. "Good old George, eh?" He looked at the limousine. "In there?"

"What'd you think, pally? You think we was taking you on a one-way tour?"

The big one said irritably: "Come on, come on. I want to get home for breakfast." With his free hand he took one of Smith's arms, urging him toward the car. The comedian who liked to talk ranged himself on the other side. A milk truck came along; its driver looked at them curiously but did not stop. The rear door of the limousine opened and the dome light came on. Smith saw that Falconer really was inside; at least a man who answered Falconer's description. He was relieved. He thought that if anything rugged or fatal had been planned, the boss would have stayed home with a lot of company to prove it.

"I'm buying a little information," Falconer said. His voice had a not unpleasant husky quality. "Would you like to get in and discuss it?" Above a dark Chesterfield and white silk muffler his face was smooth, pink, untroubled.

"Why not?" Smith climbed inside.

The car door closed behind him. Beyond it the two men lit cigarettes, engaged in desultory conversation. Their voices were muffled, indistinct.

"I'll try to make this as short as possible," Falconer said. "You're working for Van Owen?"

"I don't know," Smith said gloomily. He decided that if everybody wanted to pretend he was a private eye he might as well go along with the gag. "After what happened tonight—" He sighed. "I was supposed to prevent that sort of thing."

"But everything turned out all right, didn't it? For Miss Van Owen?"

"I suppose so. The Feds were satisfied she was being used without her knowledge."

Falconer made disparaging noises. "Just the same, it's inconvenient. Damned inconvenient. You see the spot I'm in?"

"No," Smith said, "I don't believe I do." He simply could not understand this interview. If Falconer was possessed of as much information as he seemed to be, he must surely know he was in the clear. "Unless, of course, there's a tie-in between you and the narcotics angle."

Falconer made an impatient gesture. "I wouldn't be sitting here, soldier, if there was." He offered Smith a cigar, trimmed and lit one for himself. "No, it's Van Owen I'm worried about. He swings enough weight in this town to have me closed up. If that's going to happen I'd like to know about it, that's all."

Smith looked at the broad pink face opposite him. "Why should he?"

"His daughter has come in for a lot of publicity—all this

shooting and so on." Falconer drew on his cigar, turning it slowly between thumb and two fingers. "I can see where a man in his position might get the idea all her troubles stemmed from me." His blue eyes grew bright and intent. "Has he got such an idea, soldier?"

"Could be," Smith said. "I don't think so." For the life of him he could not tell whether this was on the level or not. It was plausible. And despite all the rumors and suspicions to the contrary, Falconer could be nothing more than the big-time gambler he seemed. He remembered El Guadalupe and that gentleman's remark about a tall thin man who might or might not be connected with the Treasury Department. "Who told you about me?"

Falconer nodded as though this were a reasonable question. "I could lie to you. From what I hear, you were plenty active around that apartment house for a while, and before it was over there were enough others around so I could have got it from a dozen sources. But it was Lupe who phoned me first. That was earlier. He knew the girl was into me for some dough, and she didn't seem to like you, so he thought you might be working for me."

"Was this before or after his butcher tried to lead me out to some nice quiet cemetery?"

Falconer chuckled. "I believe he did mention some slight disagreement."

"Disagreement! If that ape ever tries anything on me again, I'll kill him." Smith opened the car door, tentatively. "Well, I'm afraid I haven't been able to tell you much you didn't know already."

"No, but you can." Falconer shifted his bulk a little, but made no attempt to detain his guest. "If Van Owen intends to start anything, let me know, will you?"

"Sure."

"There's my dough, too," Falconer said. "I'd like to get it, but I don't want to put it up to him till I know how he feels."

Smith nodded. "There's that." He opened the door wider, put one foot on the curb. "It might help if the narcotics angle were settled. You think Lupe—?"

Falconer's voice was gently reproving. "That's kind of off your beat, isn't it? I'd say it was a matter for Lupe and the Feds to argue over."

"I guess it is," Smith said. "Sorry I mentioned it." He got out.

"Good night, soldier."

Short-but-durable closed the car door. "You okay, pally? No cut throats or anything?"

"No," Smith said, "I'm fine." He drew fresh cold air deep into his lungs. "Fine." He walked toward the hotel entrance, being careful not to hurry lest they know how really frightened he had been.

Chapter 7

He dreamed that he was being wrestled around between a good angel and a bad angel, and sometimes the good angel almost had him for sure, but the wicked one was persistent and not above fouling when the occasion demanded. He himself seemed curiously unable to make up his mind which he wanted to win. The good angel, who looked a great deal like Linda, had her points. The hem of her gown was only sullied a little, and though her halo seemed made of a whitish substance, like heroin, still it was a halo, and the face beneath it was pure and kind of holy and made him wish he had led a better life.

The bad angel was more exciting, though, and infinitely more earthy. Her gown was of black and red, the lower two thirds of it suggesting the flames of hell, and her eyes glowed with a greenish light, like phosphorus in a green sea. When Linda had him and was leading him away he felt wonderful and purged of sin, but slightly regretful. But when the wicked angel pounced and her hot mouth burned his, he found sin altogether alluring and would readily have followed her down to the nethermost depths.

As sometimes happens, before one dream is resolved another is superimposed on it, and he became locked in mortal combat with a hairy ape who looked curiously like Solano, while from the sidelines El Guadalupe watched them interestedly, his womanish eyes bright and amused, his womanish body clothed in a Chinese mandarin robe of green with gold threads. He had somehow got hold of a Fu Manchu mustache, but it did not look real, whereas the ruby on his finger looked realistic as hell as the single eye of a cobra which wound its coils around one arm.

Solano's eyes were the same ruby-red; his breath was hot and rancid on Smith's face; his hands steel claws on Smith's throat. Then suddenly he was gone, and Smith seemed to be sitting in a café with George Falconer, watching a floor show, the featured attraction of which was an Indian scalping a white man. The Indian was a very fierce one and bore a marked resemblance to Captain Dietrich, and as he yanked his tomahawk out of the white man's skull Smith saw that the bloody face belonged to the youth Ralph, and that the blood was real.

He awoke screaming.

He awoke to an eleven-o'clock morning sun and a hangover to end all hangovers. There was a taste in his mouth like Solano's smell, only even a darker brown, and the sun in his eyes split his skull like Dietrich's tomahawk. He closed them again and lay back resigned to his suffering. Then he remembered the bottle Eve Dudleigh had unearthed and he opened them again. The bottle was still there. It was completely empty.

For a little while he lay perfectly quiet, considering his first move. By putting out his hand he could almost reach the telephone, and presently succor would arrive. But this involved speech, and at the moment he did not feel up to it. Besides, he did not want any of the day staff to see him as he now must look. The Smiths had their pride.

Casting back, it seemed to him that there had been more than one bottle in the secret cache; secret no longer, and probably of no value at all now, since if Eve had found it, the maid could have too. Or Cassidy.

He got up, unfolding cautiously and a little at a time, and by gripping first one chair-back, then another, finally achieved the bathroom. With a Herculean effort he lifted the lid of the flush-box. Half submerged in the water there was another bottle. Triumph glittered in his eyes and he licked his lips in anticipation. The bottle contained vermouth.

He remembered a melodrama to which his father had once, in a careless moment, taken him. The hero, a prisoner of some cut-throats aboard ship and dying of thirst, pleaded piteously for water. Handed a bottle by his sadistic tormentors, he had taken an eager swig and cried out in agony: "Sea watah!" Smith almost echoed that tragic cry.

Then it occurred to him that vermouth might have certain medicinal properties; might indeed be the very thing he needed. He lifted the bottle and drank. For a moment nothing happened. Nothing at all. Then a great deal happened, and later, much later, he was able to appreciate his good fortune in being in the most advantageous spot in the world for it.

After a time he felt better; not good, but better, and he thought he would make some coffee. He went into the small serving pantry and put the percolator on the electric plate. In the refrigerator he found a can of tomato juice and he mixed some of this with Tabasco and Worcestershire. He closed his eyes and drank the horrific concoction. It stayed down. He was tremendously gratified.

With his coffee he had a cigarette, and when there was no recurrent nausea, when his hand no longer trembled, he knew that he would live. He even began to take some interest in it.

Presently, preparing to shave, he regarded his reflection in the bathroom mirror. There were times when he thought he looked distinguished, in an evil sort of way, but this morning was not one of them. He looked disreputable. He looked as though he had been in a fight, and he suddenly remembered that he had been—indeed, two of them. The dressing applied to his neck by a coroner's physician had come loose at one end, exposing the angry red crease occasioned by Ralph's first shot. It had bled again sometime during his sleep, staining his pajamas, and he thought of how his shirt must have looked to Eve. He wondered how she possibly could have kissed him. "Maybe," he thought, "she isn't allergic to blood."

He wondered if her real reason for coming to see him was the one stated. He wondered the same thing about George Falconer and his two gorillas. He wished he had never thought what a fine, adventurous life this would be.

When he had shaved and showered and re-dressed his unheroic wound, he went into the main room and began laying out fresh clothes. He was in socks and shorts when there was a knock on the door.

It was Captain Dietrich. He came in and looked quickly about, as though expecting Smith to have company. "You alone?"

"Not now," Smith said. He did not like Dietrich. He had never liked him, but after last night, after the needless massacre of the youth Ralph, he liked him less than ever.

Dietrich must have read his mind, for he said with an approximation of apology: "I know, but there's something about a rat like that that gets me." He flushed angrily, stared at the strip of adhesive along the base of Smith's neck. "An inch or so to the left and he'd've gotten you."

Smith conceded that. It had not occurred to him before, but he was suddenly grateful to be alive, even with a hangover. He put on his shoes, shirt, and trousers. "Something particular you wanted to see me about?"

Dietrich paused in his nervous pacing. "Falconer came to see you last night." It was a statement of fact. Smith did not know how Dietrich had learned of the visit, but he had, there was no doubt of that.

Smith chose a tie, saying nothing.

"That's right, dummy up on me," Dietrich said. His short mustache seemed to bristle. "You'd think cops were a bunch of stumble-bums—or worse. But I notice you always avail yourself of our facilities when you need them, like tracing the girl last night, the one you thought you'd lost." I didn't know you guys were holding out on me? I may not be exactly sensitive, but I'm not dumb. I could feel it."

"No, you're not dumb," Smith said. He finished knotting his tie, got things from the dresser, and put them in his pockets. "If you think there's anything we know that you ought to, why don't you ask Gregg? He's the chief of this division, not me."

"Yeah, only Falconer didn't call on him; he called on you."

"Falconer thinks I'm a private dick working for Van Owen," Smith said. "At least that's what he says he thinks. If he's lying I've got somebody on the cops to thank for it."

"Or the girl," Dietrich retorted. "Or her father."

"Neither of them has any cause to love him."

"Meaning that we have?" Hot blood darkened Dietrich's already brick-red skin. "Remarks like that have been known to lose people teeth." His eyes fell away under Smith's steady stare and he said tiredly: "All right, I know he's operating inside the city limits. I know a lot of things I can't do anything about. I run the Homicide Detail."

"Sure," Smith said. He got his suit coat from the wardrobe, paused with one arm in a sleeve. "Look, maybe we can simplify this. You think we know there's someone behind the punk that knocked off Harry Gee and then got himself knocked off. You think that because Harry was one of us, in a way even a friend of mine, I'm holding out so I can take care of this guy personally. That's the usual line, isn't it?"

"What did Falconer want?"

"By God, you should have been a bulldog," Smith said admiringly. He buttoned his coat, put a fresh handkerchief in the breast pocket. "All right, I don't mind telling you. He's like you were: afraid Van Owen might put the pressure on somewhere and get him thrown out of a job."

"I'll be damned if I'm afraid!"

"Confidentially," Smith said, "I don't think Falconer is either. Not really. He just likes to protect himself in the clinches."

Dietrich looked at him steadily a moment, turned toward the door, hesitated. "You're not the easiest guy in the world to get along with, son." He sighed. "But I'm going to try." He went out.

Presently Smith too descended to the lobby and was on his way into the grill when one of the desk clerks stopped him. "This package came for you a little while ago, Mr. Smith." He had a good-sized parcel done up in heavy brown wrapping paper. Smith's name was scrawled on it in crayon, and the name of the hotel, but there was no return address, nor were there any stamps.

Smith accepted it gingerly. "How did it come?"

"Some kid brought it in. Not one of the regular parcel services."

Smith poked the thing in various spots, finally lifted it and held it to an ear. He decided it did not contain a bomb. But he was still holding his breath when he opened it and discovered nothing more lethal than a well-tailored and obviously expensive trench coat. It was, in fact, his own. He remembered that El Guadalupe had assured him it would be returned.

Chapter 8

"I do not like airplanes," Smith said, and he was certainly in a position to know whether he did or did not. He was in the cockpit of one, a border-patrol job, flying at about eight thousand feet above the uninviting and unfertile soil of Baja California. Too close to his head, a hot Mexican sun beat down on the thin metal skin of the plane's cabin. He belched in a subdued, dispirited way. A bartender had tricked him into eating the onion in his last Martini, assuring him that one would serve to neutralize the effects of the other. "Man was not intended to fly."

"Just a farm boy at heart," Cassidy said. He was on Smith's left and directly behind the pilot. He loosened his necktie, got out a handkerchief and mopped sweat from his forehead. "I always understood it was cooler the higher up you went."

"Somebody was ribbing you," Smith said. "You're closer to the sun, aren't you?" He fitted binoculars to his eyes and stared aggrievedly at the unlovely terrain spread out far below him. Cassidy and the pilot had glasses too. They were looking for a good but inconspicuous place to dump Smith when they came back that night. "I do not like being an outlaw, either. Why couldn't I be disguised as a coal-miner?"

"I don't think they have any coal mines," Cassidy said.

"I never heard of any." He addressed the pilot, a blond young man who looked as though he was barely out of high school, though he was reputed to have done some rather memorable things to the Japanese Navy. "Hey Jerry, you ever hear of any coal in Lower California?"

Jerry shook his head, no.

"Well," Smith argued, "maybe I could startle the world by finding some." Without warning he switched to Spanish, saying some very uncomplimentary things about Cassidy, Cassidy's parents, and their parents.

Cassidy's face remained placid. "You know I don't savvy that stuff."

Smith sighed heavily. "I thought you might have been holding out on the Old Man."

"Would I?" Cassidy demanded. He pretended to be overcome with indignation. "Why, this is the chance of a lifetime. You think I'd pass it up if I were fitted for the task ahead? You think I ain't dying to be one of them unsung heroes?"

The little town of Los Gatos lay beneath them now, a minuscule oasis in an otherwise barren landscape. Immediately behind it, piled-up sand dunes seemed bent on crowding it into the sea. Before it a crescent beach of hard white sand skirted an excellent harbor; a beach on which, in the old days, playboys from Hollywood and elsewhere had loved to race their leather-covered and chromium-plated cars. But the playboys went to Nevada now, or Palm Springs or Sun Valley, and the two enormous hotels that had been built in expectation of their continued favor had been allowed to go to pot. Los Gatos was Smith's target for tonight, and probably for the next few days, if not forever. He was not happy at the prospect. He felt that the gray man should undertake one of these experiments himself sometime, so that he could appreciate the true hazards his bright ideas entailed. He tried to visualize the gray man barging single-handed into a den of iniquity such as the Regans, father and daughter, were reported to be running in Los Gatos, but he couldn't. He tried to envision any good coming of it when and if he, Reed Smith, barged in on them, but he couldn't do that either.

Below them and still a long way off another plane was a silver speck in the sun. It would momentarily disappear, but when again they saw it, there was no doubt that it was growing larger and would eventually intercept them. Studying it through his binoculars, Cassidy presently identified it as belonging to the Mexican Army. "We'd better get the hell out of here."

Jerry turned his head to stare briefly at Smith. "How about setting you down on that beach tonight?"

"Sorry," Smith said, "not practicable. Not for our purposes." He sighed. "I merely quote from the Old Man's repertoire."

Jerry was indignant. "Did he ever try landing a crate belly deep in loose sand and sagebrush? In the dark?"

"No," Smith said, "but I'm sure he could. He solves all such minor problems with scarcely an effort. He does it with a pencil and paper. Besides, you're just afraid you'll have to stay down there and face a horrible death with me."

Cassidy was disgusted with them. He pointed out that the silver speck had now sprouted wings visible even to the naked eye. "We're about to be shot down for foreign spies and you guys kid around."

Jerry said he would have them. He said he didn't know why, though, since he and Smith were almost sure to die later that evening. He put the plane into a stiff bank and climb. Engine and propeller sound rose to a crescendo roar and presently the pursuing ship became a speck again, then nothing at all. They crossed the border at ten thousand feet and headed for home. Smith, occaionally as meticulous about details as the gray man would like him to be, observed that it was four fifteen.

At a quarter of five he and Cassidy were on their way into the post-office building when he heard his name called. There was quite a crowd around, last-minute purchasers of stamps and so on, but he saw Linda almost at once. She was in a rust-colored suit of silk and wool gabardine, and he noted with approval that the matching pumps had high heels. He abhorred low heels on women. "Go on up," he told Cassidy. "I'll be along in a minute." He turned a moderately pleased smile on the approaching Linda. "Hello, there!"

"I've been trying to get you all afternoon," she said.

"You have?" Over her head his eyes searched the crowd for possibly interested observers. There didn't seem to be any. "Why?"

She looked at him. "I must say you're not exactly enthusiastic."

"Well, no," he conceded. He rather ostentatiously looked at his strap watch. "Perhaps if I knew what you wanted to see me about—"

She was a trifle uncertain now, and just a little angry. "Will you have dinner with me—with us?"

"Us?"

"Father and me."

He shook his head. "I'm sorry."

"I see." She was definitely angry now. "This is the old brush, isn't it? Old but a new experience for Miss Van Owen." Her mouth curled. "Of the Van Owens, you know." Though her hat and bag were of different material they were exactly the same shade as her suit and shoes. She looked very lovely, very expensive. "Well, it's been nice knowing you, Mr. Smith." She turned away.

"Wait a minute," Smith said. "It isn't that I'm unappreciative. I'm just afraid of you, that's all."

"Afraid?" For a moment she was puzzled. Then her eyes darkened and her voice was tainted with bitterness. "You needn't have reminded me, you know. I thought of little else all night."

Smith was astonished. "Of what?"

"That it was through me a man met his death." Quite suddenly she was seized with a fit of trembling. "Two men."

"Stop that!" Smith said sharply, so sharply that two or three passers-by paused to look at them. He put an arm around her, led her to the partial seclusion of a window alcove. "Listen, give me half an hour and I'll meet you anywhere you say." He drew a deep breath. "We'll have a couple of drinks and talk this out. Okay?"

She nodded, fumbling blindly in her bag for a handkerchief. He proffered one of his and she took it, dabbing at her eyes. "I'm such an ass."

"Who isn't, these days?"

She returned the borrowed linen. "You're really quite a comfort to a gal, in an impersonal sort of way."

He put a lean brown hand under her chin, looked deep into her eyes. The golden glints were back in the irises, but she was not laughing. He was impelled to experiment with her mouth, and presently he did this, touching his lips to hers briefly, tentatively. "Is that impersonal?"

"Yes, but fairly promising." She looked past him. "We couldn't have picked a better place to play post-office, could we?" She straightened her hat. "The Cortez in half an hour, then?"

"I'll be there," he promised, and watched her out through the door and down the steps. A sleek and glistening Rolls town car drew up to the curb, a chauffeur in gray whipcord got out and helped her in. The town car went away, was swallowed up by thickening evening traffic, but Smith did not move for an unconscionably long time. In the afterglow of a dying sun his face was sharply etched, darkly brooding. He tried to conjure up a picture of Eve Dudleigh, but he could not. Linda's face, sweet, mocking, cool, arrogant, kept getting in the way. He thought that if he weren't careful he might turn out to be a very great fool. Greater, that is, than one who sold himself down the river to an unfeeling old gent named Uncle Sam. Which reminded him that one of the old gent's lieutenants, an equally unfeeling man named Gregg, was even now waiting upstairs for him. He went up.

In the main office the lights were on and there was the general bustle of any reasonably busy establishment at the close of a working day. A couple of operatives were still at their desks, bent over reports, and Cassidy was ogling a dark-haired typist while pretending to dictate a memo of vast importance, but the general trend was outward and homeward. Smith wondered how it would be to have a little woman waiting for him somewhere, bent over a pot of burned potatoes in a tiny chintzy kitchen and asking him would he please change the baby. He went in and faced the Old Man, resolved to do or die for the good of the service.

"Ah, there you are," the gray man said, and when Smith admitted that it was indeed he, leaned back in his chair, took off his pince-nez and began polishing them thoughtfully. "Do you know, it seems rather odd for all these people to be looking you up. First a Mrs. Dudleigh, whom I haven't met, then Falconer, then Captain Dietrich, and now Miss Van Owen." He looked like a mild-mannered jurist behind the over-large desk. "It's almost as though you were possessed of something, some knowledge perhaps, of which I am ignorant. Or as if they thought you were."

"You don't think it's my personal magnetism?"

"Frankly, no."

The face so like the popular conception of Mephisto's became slightly less amiable. "You're just hinting that I'm unreliable—maybe spilling my guts to somebody?"

"Quite the reverse," the gray man said. "Maybe not spilling them, in their entirety, that is, to me."

"I see." Smith pretended to find something of great interest in the palm of one hand. "Am I supposed to be doing this for money? Or, as Dietrich suggested, to pay off personally for Harry Gee?" He put suddenly enraged eyes on Gregg's face. "How would you like to get yourself a new boy?"

"I wouldn't like it," the gray man said. He sighed a little. "There have been times when you were almost like a—a son to me."

"Jesus, you're tearing my heart out."

"Well, let that go for a moment." He put his glasses back on, leaned forward. "Miss Van Owen wanted—what?"

"Didn't Cassidy tell you? He seems to have a passion lately for not minding his own business."

"Cassidy is as interested in this case as you—as we all are." Again a faint sigh escaped him. "He didn't tell me anything except that you and she had met."

"Then I'm damned if I will either," Smith said. He went over to the windows, stood looking down at the street below. The sidewalks were crowded with the rush from emptying offices; with gobs from the shore boats of the fleet; with marines from the base on North Island. "You know, I just had a funny idea: that this excursion down to Los Gatos is meant to get me out of the way for a while. What have you got in mind?"

The gray man cleared his throat. "I'm sorry if I gave you that impression; sorry too that I phrased the other matter so unfortunately. I have nothing on my mind except that this end, temporarily, is cold—for you at least. You're too well known. And you're the only man I have available who can handle the Los Gatos angle. You're a natural for it."

"All right," Smith said, "we'll pretend you've apologized." When he turned and faced the older man his eyes were no longer angry. "She's upset about last night; about Gee and her part in it. In a little while I'm going to have a drink with her at the Cortez. I may even ride around in her plush-lined town car. The condemned man ate a hearty meal before he gave his all for God and country."

"And six thousand a year," the gray man said. "Not to mention the expense account and all the drinking you do in the line of duty." From a drawer of his desk he took a thick packet of currency and a thin sheaf of what looked like bona fide newspaper clippings. He tossed the lot across to Smith. "The people likely to be interested in those probably won't know the real McSweeney, nor that he is in Alcatraz. I hope not."

"You hope not," Smith said bitterly. "Your interest in my health touches me." He saw that two or three of the fake clippings carried his own likeness. The accompanying accounts made him out a very tough character indeed. He felt that if the Regans, father and daughter, of Los Gatos, Baja California, Mexico, were really harboring wanted men, they couldn't find one more enthusiastically wanted than he.

"My informant down there," the gray man said, "is a man named Jesus Ortega. You might look him up if it seems advisable. Otherwise I have no suggestions." He stood up, nodding briskly. "Good luck, my boy."

"Thank you," Smith said. "Thank you very, very much." With his hand on the doorknob he paused. "I'm still just like a son to you?"

"Oh, yes," the gray man said. He appeared engrossed in meticulously trimming the end from one of his thin dappled cigars. "Yes indeed."

"I seem to recall another son that was sacrificed," Smith said. "That was a long time ago. I don't suppose you were his father too?"

"Don't be sacrilegious," the gray man said.

Chapter 9

The express elevator opened directly into the Sky Room, and as he stepped out, together with half a dozen other passengers, Smith saw that as usual the place was quite crowded; not packed or noisy, but full enough so that his searching eyes did not immediately find Linda. As always, the room and the atmosphere pleased him. It was a veritable gem among bars. Three sides were completely given over to plate-glass windows, through which you had a choice of looking at the bay, the open sea, the encroaching hills and mountains, the sparkling city, or the star-studded sky above it. A circular bar had a mirrored canopy over it in the form of an opening blossom, and there was plenty of chrome and black onyx in evidence, but the decorator had had a nice sense of taste and balance: the effect was not garish. Subdued lighting gave the proper accent to the view and the night beyond the windows; the service was quiet, efficient; and though there were probably a hundred different conversations going on, the sound of them was muted, pleasant. Nor was there the usual din of alleged music. You felt that you could drink for a long time here without the danger of ulcers; or, if you already had them, without inciting them to riot.

A waiter captain touched Smith's elbow. "Miss Van Owen's table is this way, sir."

The man's deference, the ease with which they negotiated passage through the well-mannered crush, gave Smith the feeling that he was about to be presented at court. He was further unnerved by finding Linda not alone. Mr. Christopher Lancaster was with her. In a dinner jacket and black tie he looked just as handsome and fit, as outdoorsy and polo-ponyish as Smith had thought him the night before.

"Hello," Linda said. "You remember Chris."

Smith said he did indeed, and the two men shook hands. "I'll be running along," Lancaster said. The laugh-crinkles at the corners of his blue eyes became accented. "Just filling in, you know. Sort of preliminary to the main event." Standing, he was not quite so tall as Smith. He smelled faintly of Russian Leather.

They chatted of this and that for a moment or two, and then some people came by who knew both Linda and Lancaster, and Smith was introduced and they all had a drink around. It was all very cozy, very chummy, and Smith felt that money must be a pleasant thing to have, though perhaps a little boring. He wondered if Lancaster knew of his sister Eve's visit last night; he wondered if Eve had reported to the police a robbery in which nothing was taken. He wondered, indeed, if she had mentioned it to Lancaster himself. It occurred to him, not for the first time, that the whole business was just something she had dreamed up on the spur of the moment, but he could not imagine why she had, or even why he felt this way.

Presently the people went away, and then Lancaster said good-night again and shook hands and returned to his own party on the other side of the room. Smith sank exhausted to a seat across from Linda. "No brass band? What kind of a reception is this?"

"Do you good," Linda said. "You lead too cloistered a life." She emptied her glass and when Smith suggested a refill she nodded. "How's your neck?"

"My neck?" He had momentarily forgotten that she had witnessed the result of his heroism, his tremendous heroism, in the battle of seven cops versus one minor mobster. He felt of his shirt collar. "Is my slip showing?"

"No, but you look tired."

"It's this mad social whirl," he said, and gratefully accepted his double Scotch from the waiter. After a time he said: "I take it that the feud is over between you and papa? The all-inclusive dinner invitation, I mean, and the town car complete with chauffeur."

Her eyes studied him across the table. In the subdued light of the room he could not see the golden glints, but certainly she was not laughing. "Tell me first why you refused the invitation. And if it wasn't what I thought, why you said you were afraid of me."

He swished the cool astringent liquor against his gums as

though to get a bad taste out of his mouth. "A slip of the tongue," he said. "I don't think we'd better go into it."

"Please don't be evasive."

"All right," he said, "if you must have it, I learned very young not to stare too long into show windows full of things I couldn't afford—that I knew my father couldn't afford." His eyes grew dark with introspection and remembrance. "There was a boat in a toy-store window once. I wanted that damned boat so bad I could taste it. I used to go back day after day and flatten my nose against the glass, and think that somehow, someday I might get it, but I never did."

"I see," she said quietly. "The parable of the boat. If it means what I think it does, I could take it as a very nice compliment. Does it?"

"Why don't we get drunk?" he suggested. He beckoned their waiter. "Let's get moderately stinking and then forget it."

"All right." But when the man had picked up the empties and gone she renewed the attack. "Has it ever occurred to you that true snobbery is not confined to the wealthy?"

He smiled at her. "Lots and lots of times. I'm trying to overcome it, though. Aren't I here drinking with you?"

"I'll tell you something else," she said. "You think my father and I are grateful for what you did—saving my life and so on. In our own clumsy way we're being nice to sort of repay the obligation." She lit a cigarette and in the brief flaming of the match he saw bright color glow high up in her cheeks. "This isn't the easiest thing I've ever said to a man, Mr. Reed Smith, but I think I've found something I need and want very badly. Am I to be denied my boat, not because I'm poor, but because I'm too damned rich?"

He shook his head. "You don't want it, not really. It's unstable, unseaworthy, and leaks like a sieve." He saw that there was a fresh glass in front of him and he seized it and drank thirstily. "You know what you are? You're a chameleon, that's what. I thought we were going to discuss your alleged guilt in relation to a couple of dead men."

"There's that too," she nodded. "You've no idea how utterly stupid and horrible I feel about it. If there were only something I could do to help—to even partially make up for—" She broke off to stare at nothing in particular for a moment. "Tell me something about your work. Is every day like yesterday?"

"God forbid," Smith said fervently. "Mostly it's pretty dull stuff and the worst you can get is ulcers. You sit around bars, maybe go to the races, hoping to get an earful that won't turn out to be somebody's dream. Oh somebody gets mad at somebody else and tips us off, or the police, and maybe we knock over some little two-bit peddler who doesn't know anything and wouldn't tell us if he did." Again he beckoned the waiter to come and replenish their glasses. It occurred to him that he was beginning to verge on that moderately stinking state he had threatened, but Linda was apparently unaffected. "What're you doing, pouring yours out the window?"

She said no, the stuff just didn't seem to take hold tonight. This time it was she who drank with apparent thirst. "You make it all sound pretty uninteresting. Don't you ever beat these—these people who won't tell you anything?"

Smith shook his head sadly. "They won't let us. Our tyrant bosses, I mean. We're supposed to be gentlemen. We got culture."

"Oh?"

"You bet," he said. "Now take me, I got culture like anything." He lifted his glass and sipped daintily, to show her how cultured he was. "Madame, would you care to join me in a hamburger or some such tasty morsel? I know a joint up the coast road that is frequented by our very best truck-drivers."

"Now you're just showing off."

"No," he said, "really. I'll bet you've got a fur rug in that town car of yours. I yearn to put my feet in it." He stood up and with some little difficulty balanced himself disdaining the change from a twenty-dollar bill proffered him by the waiter. "No, no, my good man. I too know what it is to suffer under the heels of tyrants." He offered a gallant arm to Linda. "Madame?"

They rode down in an elevator filled with nice, opulent-smelling people, and presently, debouching from the lobby, waited under the marquee while Linda's car was called. The night had turned cooler, and a light fog was coming in from the sea. The fresh air had a tonic effect on Smith, diluting the faint haze occasioned by too much Scotch too fast. When the Rolls came up he discovered that he hardly had to lean on Linda at all. He felt fine. He felt even better when he discovered that there really was a fur rug on the tonneau floor. It proved that his powers of deduction were unimpaired, were indeed even sharpened by the judicious use of Scotch. He thought that if he cared to he might become a very great detective indeed.

As the car got under way he directed Linda, who in turn directed the chauffeur, a middle-aged man named Jenkins, to their destination. He leaned back and from beneath half-lowered lids regarded Linda's profile. "How many people have you told about me, precious?"

"About you?" With the night, she had turned cooler, or so it now seemed to him. "How do you mean?"

"Am I still a private eye, or am I being spoken of in my true character?" There were fresh violets in a cut-glass and silver vase and he inhaled appreciatively. "Lancaster, for instance. Did you happen to tell him the kind of work I work at when I work?"

She looked at him. "What has Chris got to do with it? And anyway, I didn't. I'm not quite a fool."

"Oh, but you are," he insisted. "If you weren't you wouldn't be on your way to nibble a hamburger with the proletariat. How about Lancaster's sister?"

"Eve?" She seemed genuinely startled. "Don't tell me you're interested in her!"

"I could be," he said. He made luscious sounds with his lips.

She drew a little farther away from him. "So she has that effect on you too." And after a time: "I thought it was just my money you didn't like. It's nice to know that even without it I wouldn't exactly set you afire."

"That's the trouble with us commoners," Smith said. "We aren't subtle. We don't know how to tell a gal off without hurting her feelings." He leaned toward her. "Can I help it if I dreamed about you last night, and you were so pure and kind of holy I just couldn't bear to take advantage of your innocence?"

"You didn't!"

"Sure I did." He did not tell her that the dream also included Eve Dudleigh. "You were an angel, complete with halo."

"Imagine that." Then she said: "Dear God," and laughed a little, and turned and seized his face in her two hands and kissed him. He was impressed. He was more than that. He was considerably shaken, and presently he discovered that it was he, not she, who sought a continuance of the embrace. She withdrew from him a little, and he saw that her eyes had grown larger and glowed with a catlike intensity. "The halo still there, darling?"

"It's fading," he admitted. He put his arms around her. "Perhaps another application—"

After a time she said: "Reed?"

"Yes, precious?"

"What became of my gun—the one you took away from me last evening?"

He was indignant. "At a time like this she talks about guns!"

"No, I'm serious. You still have it?"

He felt that a small lie was in order. "But of course. I'm going to keep it too, till I'm sure you've reformed."

With apparent irrelevance she asked if he had been back to Tia Juana since last night, and when he said no, he hadn't, she said that he and truth were obviously unacquainted. "My gun was in the pocket of the trench coat you checked at Lupe's casino. When we left there you didn't have your coat."

"But I did have a gun, remember?"

"Not mine."

"What an observant wench it is!" he said tenderly. "I will now confound your logic with the information that Lupe returned my coat this morning."

She was incredulous. "With my gun in it?"

"Certainly."

"This I will have to see," she said, and unhooked the tiny microphone. "Jenkins, will you please drive back to—"

"Never mind," Smith said sadly. "I'll confess. I threw it down a drain."

"Now I know you're lying!"

"But you can't prove it," Smith said. "It was a very deep drain."

Chapter 10

The lights of the city fell away swiftly and were swallowed up beneath the cloak of light ground fog, and then there was nothing but Smith and Jerry the pilot and the little plane and the night. The drone of the engine was a lullaby, sweetly plaintive as the humming of a giant Negro chorus, courting sleep. Smith earnestly hoped that Jerry would not go to sleep. They were heading straight out to sea.

Jerry was still complaining about the hazards of landing among sand dunes, sagebrush, and one thing and another. "Why don't you just let me dump you out with a chute?"

"Me?" Smith said. "A chute?" He shuddered at the thought. "Thank you, no." He focused his eyes on the lighted instrument panel because there was nothing else to look at. He couldn't even see the wing tips any more. They were flying dark. Just to make conversation he pretended to be very interested in the science of aeronautics and navigation.

"How can you tell we won't end up in China?"

Jerry explained how he could tell. He did this rather

sketchily, no doubt believing that Smith couldn't have got through college without mastering the rudiments of mathematics, but in this he was wrong. College, to Smith, was a place where they played basket ball. After a time he thanked Jerry politely and appeared to be vastly relieved. It seemed that the general idea was to fly so many miles out into the Pacific, then so many miles south, then east again on a new course, executing a reasonably horizontal U-shaped maneuver which would eventually bring them to where they wanted to go without encountering either the planes of their own border patrol or others to whom explaining would be even more difficult. Smith wondered idly why the same tactics employed in reverse wouldn't work equally well for an organized narcotics ring, and Jerry said not to think they hadn't been employed, only it was a little tougher going the other way.

"The big problem is landing," Jerry said. "There aren't so very many places on our side, and those are all under surveillance. Not that they don't try. We've had several brushes with an unidentified plane lately. Maybe more than one."

Smith nodded approval of the border patrol's efficiency and went to sleep. This time he dreamed of dead men with leering mouths and sightless eyes, like zombies, who were trying to wrest Linda from his arms. He awakened to find that it was only Jerry shaking him and wanting to know what the hell was the matter. "Los Gatos," Jerry said, pointing.

With the palms of his hands Smith rubbed sleep from his eyes and obediently looked downward. The fog had thinned now, and the little town lay like a jeweled crescent along the curve of broad white beach. In the harbor the riding lights of a dozen small craft rose and fell against the blackness of the sea. For the first time he was conscious of the cessation of all sound. They were flying with a dead stick. Smith wished he were back with the zombies. "Thank you for waking me," he said. "I wouldn't have missed this sight for anything. Not for anything."

"I wasn't shilling for the beauties of the place," Jerry said. "I just didn't want you to bite your tongue off when we hit." As they lost altitude and the hills back of Los Gatos enfolded them he said: "You savvy how to set off the flares?"

"Oh yes," Smith said. "Yes indeed. I used to be a Boy Scout." He saw that Jerry was unimpressed. "I was an Eagle Scout."

"Well, I'll be somewhere around, every night at this same time," Jerry said, adding that he would if he lived to get off the ground after the now imminent landing.

Smith looked at his watch, saw that it was eleven fifteen. The plane's right wing tip scraped the top off a sand dune, then they were down with a tremendous rocking and bumping of the wheels. But at least they were down. Smith sighed relievedly. "Good old terra firma."

Jerry cursed. "Terra firma. I'm hub-deep in sand, by God!" Without happiness, but without envy either, he watched Smith untangle his long legs and make a crablike exit. "Don't light those flares unless you really need me, chum."

Smith looked at him. "I don't even celebrate the Fourth of July any more." He surveyed the immediate vicinity, a shallow depression in the midst of barren hills, with patent disfavor. "Which way would you suggest I go from here?"

Jerry waved a casual fist. "Over thataway, pardner. I think there's a road about half a mile over."

"That won't be much help," Smith prophesied darkly. "Not if I know Mexican roads."

Jerry got out to look at his wheels and estimate his run, and they stood there a moment, listening. There was not a sound. The blackness of the night shrouded them, thick as a blanket, and the vague shapes of the dunes seemed to be creeping in on them, confident, unhurried, menacing. Jerry shivered. "Well, it's been nice knowing you, pal." He climbed back into the plane, the door thudded shut. There was the plaintive whine of the starter, a swiftly muffled roar as the engine caught, then the sand-clogged wheels began to roll. Jerry waved a farewell salute; then he really gunned the throttle, and Smith was knocked flat by a hurricane composed of equal parts of wind and sand.

After a while he sat up and he was alone, with nothing to remind him that Jerry and the plane had ever been there but the paper-wrapped parcel of magnesium flares. It took him the better part of half an hour to locate the road and to bury the package beside it, but he was in no great hurry now. Humming the *Song of the Marines,* he emptied his shoes of sand and started slogging toward where he thought Los Gatos ought to be. He was quite sure he would never signal Jerry down from the skies, because he didn't think he could again find the spot where he had buried the flares.

The road was an uncompromising thing. Instead of skirting some of the miniature mountains impeding its progress, it persisted in climbing to the very tops and then diving steeply, only to climb again. Rutted, strewn with rock, it was not an ideal path to negotiate on foot. Smith was limp and discouraged when, after the second or third ascent, there was still no heartening glow in the sky to herald the near presence of Los Gatos.

Breathing gustily, and muttering blasphemies against the gray man for having thought up this idea, he slid down the next declivity on his heels, making quite a clatter because of the loose rock and rubble underfoot. He came upon the car quite suddenly. One moment he was alone in the desert, a pioneer, an orphan. The next, rounding a huge pile of boulders, he was face to face with direct evidence of another's presence.

A faint glow emanated from the instrument panel, enough to show him that the car was empty, but that did not necessarily mean that the car's owner was not somewhere close at hand. He stood very still for an instant, debating whether to retrace his steps, to ignore the car and go on, or to give his feet a break and utilize the vehicle, come what might. He finally decided on the latter course and approached the car boldly.

A woman's voice said: "Stay where you are!" The woman herself rose from the far side and Smith saw that she had a gun. He stayed where he was. Looking beyond the gun he was unable to make out minute details, but it was almost certain that no woman with a voice like that could be anything but beautiful. "Sure," he said. "Anything you say, beautiful."

"I heard you coming," she said.

He nodded ruefully. "Unless you were stone-deaf you couldn't miss. Club-footed elephants couldn't have done better."

She appeared to think that over for a moment. Then, not in the least nervous, merely curious, she said: "You're a stranger around here, aren't you?"

"I sure am, pardner." He looked down at his scuffed shoes. "I could go even farther and say I'm sorry I ever heard of this spot."

She jerked the gun in a small, imperative gesture. "Come around in front of the headlights." And when he did this she reached her left hand inside the car and snapped a switch. In the ensuing glare Smith thought that probably she could see the mole under his left shoulder blade. Certainly she detected the bulge beneath his coat lapel, for she said: "I see you carry a gun, stranger."

He shrugged. "One never knows whom one will meet."

"I don't remember passing you on the road."

"That's funny," he said. "It seems like I've been on it for hours." He had the curious feeling that if she had ever been, she was no longer afraid of him. Her questions were not exactly the type engendered by fear.

She put another one. "Have you a passport?"

"Well, no," he said easily. "The truth of the matter is, I seem to have mislaid it somewhere. I thought that possibly, in Los Gatos—"

"Turn around," she said suddenly. And when his back was to her: "Now drop your gun." He could hear her quick indrawn breath. "And do be careful, friend. I'm supposed to be a pretty fair shot."

"I haven't a doubt of it," he assured her earnestly. "You appear to be a most competent young lady in every respect. Beautiful, too," he added as he removed the automatic from his shoulder holster and laid it gently on the ground. Presently, receiving her permission, he turned and discovered that she also was now outlined in the glare of the headlights. He saw that his first impression was fully justified. She was beautiful as hell. At another time he might have thought himself fortunate indeed to have met so many really lovely women in so short a span as two days. And well-assorted, too. This one's hair was darkly red under a modish little hat that on anyone else he would have considered ridiculous. Her suit was of some sleek blue-gray material and strictly not the kind of suit you saw by the dozen in somebody's bargain basement. It molded, or perhaps was molded by, a body that so far as he could see was without flaw. Her eyes seemed to be of the same color as the suit, blue-gray. They were faintly amused as they met the admiration in his. "I thought I heard a plane a little while ago."

"You did?"

She laughed then, throatily, and something about the sound, or the way she stood, reminded him of Eve Dudleigh. The two women were utterly dissimilar in appearance, but each had that quality which is sometimes referred to as physical magnetism. "They certainly couldn't hang you for anything you've told me so far," she said. "You afraid of talking, or is that just the way you are?"

"It's my disposition," he said. "I'm what's known as a taciturn fellow. Maybe churlish would be better." With his thumb and forefinger he flipped the pebble he had picked up when depositing his gun. It was a great surprise to her. It caught her just over the bridge of her very nice nose and so confused her that her pistol was at least a foot out of line when she squeezed the trigger. The single explosion was still racketing around the hills when he moved in and chopped down on her wrist with the hard edge of his hand. The pistol clunked to the ground. "Now," he said amiably, "now we can be really comfortable. We can settle down for a nice quiet friendly chat."

For a long moment she just stared at him, her left hand massaging what must have been a rather painful right wrist. Then, surprisingly, she laughed. "I like smart guys," she said. She stepped backward toward the car, carefully, as he bent and picked up both guns. "You wouldn't be smart enough to fix a flat without a jack, would you?" She said a most unladylike word. "This makes three I've had stolen in the last six months."

Smith was genuinely sympathetic, although more than a little apprehensive at the prospect of work. "You can't trust anybody these days. Especially in Mexico." He stowed the guns away, his own in its holster, hers in a pants pocket. It seemed to him that he was spending his life doing nothing but disarming people who wanted to shoot him. It was getting monotonous. Dangerous, too. "At least that's what I've heard," he said, and added a terrific lie to his other sins. "This is my first trip, and except for meeting you I wish I'd never made it."

"You'll learn to love it," she said, not without a trace of irony, and together they went around and looked at the flat.

Smith in particular found the sight depressing, but negotiating that rocky road on a tireless rim was even more so. He decided it was not only impractical, it was impossible. He sighed heavily. "Well, for such a nice girl I suppose I could even change a tire."

"I could go for you too," she said with charming frankness. "Incidentally, my name is Regan, Juanita Regan. I don't know why the Juanita, except that my mother was an incurable romantic. She read paper-backed novels."

Smith bowed from the waist, very courtly. "Smith," he said. "I come from a long line of Smiths, all expert tire-changers." He reached inside the car and released the emergency brake. There was a slight grade at this point and the car began rolling backward. All he had to do was guide it till the rear right-hand wheel hung suspended over the ditch beside the road.

Miss Regan supplied the necessary tools for the wheel change. "You're a funny guy," she said.

"I'm a card," he said, tightening the last lug. He thought it was quite a coincidence that of all the ladies in Baja California, the one whose activities he was supposed to investigate should be the very first he encountered. "Could you tell me the way to a town named Los Gatos?"

"You can ride in with me," she said. "I live there."

"You do?" He pretended to be vastly surprised. "That ought to make it more endurable for the rest of the populace." He put the extra wheel in the rumble. "Quiet place?"

"Not very," she admitted. He could feel her blue-gray eyes probing him. "You looking for a quiet place?"

"Kind of."

"Got any money?"

He straightened, his face undergoing some subtle change that made it infinitely evil and menacing. For the first time she appeared the least bit frightened. "I might know where there is some," he said. He took a step toward her, his leer a shameful thing, born of that personage he most resembled. "Are you as greedy as you sound, pet?"

"Just practical," she said shortly. There was a swish of modish skirt, then she was inside the car and behind the wheel. "Come on, I won't charge you anything for the lift."

"Now, that's right generous of you, pardner." He got in beside her, his knees as usual bumping the dash. "Our garage gives free midnight service, too."

They rumbled and roared and bumped and swayed along the road for almost a mile before she spoke again. Then she said: "If you've got money, and you're interested in a quiet place—a very quiet place—you might try the Casa de las Dos Palmas."

"Thank you," he said gravely. "I'll remember that: the Dos Palmas." After a while he said tenderly: "I'll remember you too, baby." Then, to show her how sorry he was for that horrific leer; how he was really a gentleman at heart, unless you aroused his baser instincts, he took her gun from his pocket and laid it on the ledge above the instrument panel.

Chapter 11

They gave him a second-floor room and presently, stripped down to undershirt and shorts, he was arguing in Spanish with the mestizo who passed for a valet at the Dos Palmas. "No, I do not wish to sell the suit. I desire only that it shall be brushed and pressed."

"*Sí. Gracias, señor.*"

"And thanks to you too," Smith said politely. He waited for the mestizo to go away, but apparently the youth was in no hurry. He stared with naïve admiration at the length of Smith's legs; he exhibited interest in the strip of adhesive along the base of Smith's neck. "You are here for long, no?"

"For long, no," Smith said. He went into the bath and turned on the shower. When he looked out the door, the mestizo was examining the automatic slung in its harness on the bedpost. "Put it down, *muchacho.*"

Reluctantly the youth put it down. "It is very beautiful, that one." He pointed a not too clean index finger at Smith's chest and waggled the attached thumb. "Boom!" he said.

"Oiga!" Smith's tone was severe. "I do not desire that we should play Indian. I am in a very great hurry for that suit. Now scram. *Andale!*"

The mestizo gave up. He even decided there was no use continuing the mild deception that he couldn't understand English. "Hokay," he said. He went away, carrying Smith's only available suit.

Smith again repaired to the bath and with the fine stream beating the dust from his lank frame turned his mind to the problem at hand. He was in Los Gatos, but for how long he would be permitted to remain he did not know. There was always a catch to it somewhere, he thought sadly. If he had crossed the border in the usual manner, with either a passport or a temporary permit, the fiction of his being a fugitive from justice would have sounded improbable. He would immediately have been open to suspicion by the very people he was trying to impress with his lawlessness. But this way he was open to suspicion by *el policía.*

He wondered if the Mexican cops were aware of him yet. He almost hoped they were, because interrogation by them, possibly a threatened deportation, would perhaps draw the attention of those whose attention he wished to attract. On the other hand, the authorities could make it very tough indeed in case they discovered that he was wanted in the United States. He had no desire for even a brief sojourn in a Mexican jail. The memory of three whole days in the *cárcel* at Nogales was still with him.

He thought of the gray man without love, and of Cassidy, whom he envied, because Cassidy wouldn't have to drink tequila, and he thought, a very little, about Linda. Toweling himself vigorously he considered the beautiful and mercenary Juanita Regan. On the whole he was glad he had met her when he had, not only because meeting her thus had saved him a long walk, but because investigating her and her associates, if any, promised to be an interesting chore. He could not recall his last experience with a redhead, but he was sure that never before had he seen red hair so richly dark and lustrous.

And as for her recommendation of the Hotel de las Dos

Palmas, she certainly was not given to exaggeration. The sprawling two-storied stucco-and-tile building was quiet. It was so quiet it almost hurt your ears. One whole wing had been completely blocked off, its windows boarded up; and even the part that was open for business had an air of distress, of decaying magnificence, of an enterprise on the verge of collapse.

Smith re-entered the bedroom, intending to wrap himself in a blanket as a makeshift robe until his suit was returned. There was a man standing at the dresser. He gave no sign that Smith's abrupt entry embarrassed him.

"I'm Regan," he said. He might have posed for the original of McManus's famous Jiggs. Short thick legs supported a heavy, squat body, and the squarish bulldog face was surmounted by a pate bald as an egg except for the traditional fringe of stiff reddish hair. The big difference between this man who called himself Regan and the cartoon character lay in the eyes. There was no humor in Regan's. They were bright and green and crystal-hard.

Smith examined the squat body for a bulge that would indicate a concealed gun. He measured the distance between himself and the bedpost where hung his shoulder harness. He thought that if necessary he could make it before Regan could. "All right," he said calmly, "so you're Regan. Does that entitle you to come in without knocking?"

"The name don't mean anything to you?"

"It means I've met a gal using the same one." Smith made his voice deliberately insulting. "You can't be related, though. She's too good-looking."

Angry color suffused the broad, bulldog face. "Down here I'm a kind of king, brother. It'll pay you to get along with me."

"Maybe you only think you're a king," Smith said. He wondered if Regan had located the faked clippings yet. "I never heard of you, myself." Without apparent hurry he moved over to the bed, sat on it, and wrestled his undershirt over his head. Through the thin mesh he watched his visitor, but Regan only stood there, unblinking, immobile as the Sphinx. Smith put on his shorts, then his socks and shoes. Regan's eyes and the prolonged silence were beginning to tell on him, though. "Nope," he said, "never heard of you."

"I thought you might have," Regan said. "I run the Dos Palmas for the syndicate that started it."

"Oh?" Smith scowled at the grime on his only shirt. "Then maybe you can tell me where I could buy a shirt at this time of night. And hurry up that mestizo with my pants."

"A shirt will cost you twenty dollars, brother."

Smith shook his head. "Not my brand of shirts. I wear the four-buck kind."

"That's the kind I'm selling for twenty," Regan said. He massaged his blunt, outthrust jaw with a powerful hand. Reddish hair grew clear down to the second joints of his spatulate fingers. "Unless, that is, you have a passport. Or a temporary."

Rage darkened Smith's face. He stood up, his eyes glowing. "You're a lousy, two-bit chiseling son of a bitch. So she told you that, did she?"

"Sure she told me." Regan's sudden grin was like the wolf's in *Little Red Ridinghood.* "I'm trying to give you a break, sucker, on account of you gave the kid an assist. For half a grand I might even fix you up with a permit."

"You touch me," Smith said. "But not for half a grand. Also I will wear my old shirt for a while." He snapped his gun out of the clip and centered it on Regan's paunch. "Now, you cheap bastard, get on that phone before I blow you in two. I want my pants."

The self-styled king of Los Gatos, like his daughter, did not scare easily. "Okay, sucker, you'll learn." He moved to the phone and spoke into it in awkward, uncomfortable Spanish. Then, hanging up, he turned to regard Smith with the disinterest an entomologist accords the ordinary or garden variety of butterfly. "Some it takes longer than others, but you'll learn." When presently there was a knock on the door, he opened it and the mestizo came in with the rejuvenated suit.

Smith wore the unhappy expression of a man who is stuck and knows it. "All right, chiseler, how much for pressing the suit?"

"Whatever you want to give him," Regan said. His paunch shook with sudden mirth; a sort of gravelly sound came out of his mouth. "I'm not a hog." He went out.

"The hell he's not a hog," Smith said to the mestizo.

"Ees very fonny man, that wan," the youth said. He looked at Smith's face, at the gun still held foolishly in Smith's hand. "Ees laugh like that w'en twisting in you the knife." He drew a suggestive finger across his throat. Then abruptly his smile died and quite unashamedly he crossed himself.

Chapter 12

Descending to the lobby a half hour later, fully dressed and rather pleased with an effect he had created in his room, Smith found no one there but the desk clerk he had seen when registering. The three or four nondescript guests in evidence earlier had either retired or departed for livelier spots. He decided that even in Los Gatos and at one thirty in the morning there must be livelier ones; there could hardly be any that were deader. He was sorry that old Shylock Regan wasn't around to see him venturing forth without benefit of papers, real or forged, with which to propitiate the local constabulary. He put a trace of swagger into his walk, to impress the clerk, but the man only nodded and returned to his perusal of *Hoy*.

Outside, he discovered that, though clear, the night had turned quite chilly and he wished that he had brought along a topcoat. Still, a guy on the lam mustn't look too prosperous and comfortable. Besides, the chill was an even better excuse than thirst or business for hoisting a few drinks. Going down the drive, he observed again the ragged lawns and untrimmed hedges and trees, the weed-grown flower beds. Not for the first time, it occurred to him that Mexico might have done better without its sudden moral upsurge in the matter of legalized gambling. His sympathies were all with the syndicate whose million-dollar investment was rotting away. He considered writing them a letter suggesting that their majordomo, Señor Regan, might better be employed with a hoe than selling four-dollar shirts to outlaws for twenty. As he approached the brighter lights along the Avenida Juan Batista he saw what he had already suspected, that Los Gatos was strictly a one-street town. The three or four cross-streets were hardly worthy of the name, being little more than rocky, unpaved lanes with no purpose other than to bisect twin rows of more or less dilapidated dwellings. Each of these cross-roads terminated abruptly in cactus-covered desert, like anemic streams that, giving up the struggle at last, sink to oblivion in greedy sands.

Furtive figures came and went along these unlighted byways, deeper shadows in the gloom, and such houses as showed any light at all were heavily shuttered from prying eyes. The smell of the sea, laden with the odors of fish and drying kelp and oil-slick from the boats in the harbor, was blown inland on a rising breeze. Here and there along the grandiloquently named avenue a neon sign advertised a touch of night life, if you were interested, and the strains of *La Golondrina* issued from a juke box in the nearest cantina. Off to the left, set smack in the middle of the desert, was a rather pretentious array of stucco buildings dominated by a brightly lit revolving windmill. Enormous neon letters spelled out *"El Molino Rojo."* Apparently the current administration considered only gambling a vice. A number of cars were parked around the Mill, a few up and down the Avenue of John the Baptist, who, Smith felt, would have been displeased with what Los Gatos had done to him.

He paused for a moment before the window of a closed haberdashery, pretending an interest in the array of ties, shirts, and socks. He could have used one of the shirts at that, but the tiny shop next door, also closed, was the real focal point of his attention. Flaking machine-made gilt letters on the glass proclaimed that here one could buy tobaccos, stationery, and all the latest periodicals. The showcase inside was piled with boxes of dusty-looking cigars and mounds of cigarette packages, some of them imitating Camels, Chesterfields, and Luckies, but all filled, as Smith knew from sad experience, with the same acrid Mexican fodder. He was not ready yet to interview J. Ortega, Proprietor, but he was glad to know where to find him, when and if the time came. He wondered why Jesus Ortega had turned stool-pigeon. The gray man had not told him that. Perhaps he didn't know.

He crossed the street and went through the door from which *La Golondrina* still issued. Besides himself and the bartender there were six men in the place. Five of them were Mexicans. The sixth was a white man, but he had long since forgotten it. He was dirty and unkempt and his sockless feet showed through rents in his shoes. He nursed a bottle of tequila furtively, as though afraid the others would take it from him if they knew he had it.

Smith stood at the end of the bar nearest the door and looked at the bartender. "Scotch?" he said without conviction.

The barkeep was a swart, paunchy man with oily handlebar mustaches and a knife scar puckering one fat cheek. He considered Smith's question for a long moment. Then his mustaches moved upward and outward in what was probably meant for a smile, but looked as though he were about to spit through his teeth. "Tequila."

"No rye, either?"

"Tequila," the man said. It was final.

Smith nodded unhappily. "I'll take tequila."

The five Mexicans were now all at one table. Certain that Smith could not understand them, or perhaps not caring, they discussed him at great length. There was some dissension over his exact height. One said that he was taller than a horse's head, though this was considered an exaggeration by the others.

"He has a cunning look, that one."

"But clumsy."

"Sí." They all laughed.

Smith saw that there was no use asking for such effete things as salt and lemon to take the curse off the tequila. He closed his eyes so he couldn't see what he was doing to his stomach and tossed off three fingers of liquid fire, of molten glass flavored slightly with anise. "Great stuff," he said when he could speak again.

"Pay now," the barkeep said.

Smith could see he wasn't going to make friends and influence people in this dive. He laid a dollar on the bar, waved the change away, and sought the fresh air of the Avenida Juan Batista. He was halfway down the almost deserted block when he heard shuffling footsteps behind him, and a whine. "Wait a minute, neighbor." It was the bum from the cantina. Bleary eyes peered cunningly up at Smith's face. "How's about a couple pesos for a fellow countryman?"

"Scram," Smith said. He felt that he should be getting into character as Twister McSweeney, a very tough number indeed. "Go lay it in an alley some place."

The bum recoiled, but only a little. "I think I seen you somewhere before, pally." His eyes became slits and his mouth leered loosely. "In Juárez, maybe?"

"Maybe. I've been in Juárez."

The bum cackled. "I knew it. Never forget a face." His forehead wrinkled and again his eyes were slits, this time in a tremendous effort to concentrate. "Let's see now, that was about the time the Gonzalez mob was busted up."

Smith was glad he had had the tequila; this guy's befuddled memory was coming very close to him. "Yeah," he said, "and so what's it to you?"

"How about a fin, pally?"

Smith got a handful of dirty shirt and ragged coat lapels, bunching them under the drunk's chin. "Look, bud, I did my stretch in Atlanta for that one. You still want to play funny?"

The whine again. "Hey, I didn't mean nothin'!"

"Well, don't, see?" Smith shook him once, released him. "Where can a guy pick up a fast bindle or two down here?"

The bum straightened himself with offended dignity. Grimy hands brushed at his lapels. "You on the habit?"

"Christ no," Smith said. "I feed the stuff to my pet mice." He jingled the silver in a trousers pocket. "You want a buck or don't you?"

"Somebody over at the Red Mill ought to take care of you," the bum said. He licked his lips. His eyes slid away from Smith's.

"Somebody better," Smith told him, "or I'll come back and kick your face in." He threw a silver dollar down the sidewalk, watched the drunk skitter after it, fall on it, get up, and scuttle through the door of the cantina. Then, with eyes that were not particularly happy, suddenly conscious that he'd just been through a somewhat nerve-racking experience, he went down the street till he identified one of the parked cars as a makeshift taxi. Presently, behind a native driver who didn't know his own strength, he went bucketing off across the desert. The tequila glowed warm and friendly in his stomach.

Close up, El Molino Rojo presented the liveliest front of anything Smith had seen below the border since the old days when from the Gulf of Mexico to the Pacific the cities and towns along it ran wide open. The main building and the two neat rows of stucco cribs gleamed whitely against the greenery of an artificial oasis, and the tall, slowly revolving arms of the neon-lighted fan cast an illusion of movement over the whole. There were more cars around than he had thought. Invisible from the town side, the parking area marked off by whitewashed boulders was nearly half full. From behind drawn blinds in the nearest cubicle came the sound of a woman's brittle laughter. Beyond the wide-open doors of the main entrance there were music and the stamp of boisterous dancing feet.

He took his gun out of the shoulder clip and put it in a trousers pocket. Then, instructing his somnolent charioteer to wait for him, he went inside. A Mexican girl in an abbreviated red dress took his hat. She had a great jeweled Spanish comb in her hair and Smith patted her cheek and told her how beautiful she was. "*Magnífico!*"

Her smile became a trifle less mechanical. "You are a stranger here, señor."

This seemed to be a stock observation tonight. "*Sí,*" he admitted, and went and stood by the inner doors and studied the crowd inside. A dozen or more couples swayed and galloped about the dance floor. There were only three or four white men. The girls were all Mexican. Around the walls were small curtained booths, the closed curtains of many indicating that they were occupied. He became more cheerful as he saw that the bar sported an array of bottles that would have done credit to any bistro in San Diego. The only trouble was that there were too many unescorted girls between him and the bottles. He had no desire to run the gantlet of clutching hands and toothy smiles just to get a drink. He chose one of the empty booths instead.

A waiter in a reasonably clean apron paused beside the table. Like the bartender in the other dive this man too had a knife scar. They seemed to like to live dangerously in Los Gatos. "Scotch," Smith said. "Double." The waiter went away. Smith, in full view of the room but with an air of furtiveness, took from an inner coat pocket a small fold of white paper, dumped its contents on the back of a hand and flipped the hand to his nostrils. He pretended to be very angry when the returning waiter caught him at it. "So what the hell are you gawking at?" He brushed crystals of pure cane sugar from a coat lapel.

"Nothing, señor." He set Smith's drink down, collected a dollar for it, and departed. A parade of girls began passing the booth, some coy, some brazen, but all of them open to the least little suggestion that Smith was lonely. He scowled at them, sipping his drink in sullen solitude.

After a while a dapper little man in a plaid suit and a derby slid into the seat opposite him. He looked like a racetrack tout. With a kind of legerdemain, like a magician, he produced a handful of postcards, fanning them out for Smith's inspection. They were of the type known as "French," though these were Central or South American and even worse. "You in the market, brother?"

"Not for that garbage," Smith said.

"For something else, then? Maybe some—powder?"

Smith looked at the wizened, greedy face. "What's your monicker, punk?"

"Cagy."

Smith nodded. "Maybe I'll be seeing you around."

"Just ask anybody," the small man said. He slid out of the booth and disappeared as quietly as he had come.

The orchestra banged on and on; feet stomped; women laughed shrilly, artificially. There was a miasma of assorted smells, liquor and beer and smoke and sweat and bodies too heavily powdered. Presently Smith ordered a second drink. He was in the middle of this when a tall handsome Mex in the uniform of the constabulary came through the front doors. His insignia said he was a captain. Smith was not too surprised when the newcomer clicked spurred heels across the dance floor and came to rest immediately before the booth. "I am of *el policía,* señor." He translated. "Of the police."

Smith waved a hand. "Have a drink."

"Thank you, no." *El capitán* frowned. He was proud of his military carriage. "I am Captain Hernandez."

Smith gave his own name with the feeling that Hernandez already knew. "What's on your mind?"

Eyes bright and shiny as jet probed Smith's face. "You do not come in on the boat, señor?" And when Smith shook his head: "Nor do you possess a car?"

Smith admitted that he did not possess a car.

"Then how do you arrive in Los Gatos, señor?"

Smith had been considering this eventuality for some little time now. After observing the town in detail he hadn't believed it possible to go walking around for long without some sort of questioning. "I came over from Tia Juana in a taxi," he said. "It broke down and I started to walk. Finally I got a ride in with a lady named Juanita Regan."

Hernandez's expression said that he had already checked Smith as far back as the ride with the girl. It was doubtful that she had described the exact circumstances, especially if influenced by her father, but in all this Smith was able to sense Regan's fine, Machiavellian hand. This was the prelude to the bite. Hernandez hooked a thumb in his Sam Browne belt. It was done casually, but his fingers were very close to the holstered pistol. "You have the passport, perhaps? Or the permit?"

Smith said of course, certainly he had a permit, he had it right here. He made a great business of looking for it, allowing Hernandez to see that his shoulder clip was innocently empty. He was astonished when his search was fruitless. "By God," he said, "I must have left it in my room!"

El capitán spread his hands. "These things will happen, no?" He looked at his wrist watch. "For tonight I trouble you no more, so. But in the morning you will bring to me this permit, eh?"

"Absolutely," Smith said. "You can count on it." He was furious, not so much because of the squeeze, but because they didn't give a damn how obvious it was. Nevertheless, he felt that he had made considerable progress in his first couple of hours in town. He watched Hernandez leave, a handsome and debonair *caballero* who was honoring his country by wearing its uniform. He waited perhaps ten minutes more, just in case anybody should think he was nervous. Then he got up and went out to his dilapidated taxi and was driven back to the hotel of the two palms.

Regan himself was behind the desk this time. "Hi, sucker."

"Leech," Smith said. He leaned his elbows on the counter, regarded the red, bulldog face with elaborate admiration. "The price on bootleg permits still the same?"

"I ought to boost it a little," Regan said. He sighed, heavily. "But a deal is a deal. I'll let the half grand ride."

"White of you," Smith said. He peeled five hundred-dollar bills from his roll. "I'm going to need one in the morning."

"I thought you would," Regan said.

Chapter 13

Smith's carefully prepared plant had been disturbed. That was the first thing he discovered on entering his room. There were not quite so many flakes of paper ash scattered about the bath, and looking under the lavatory he saw that the clipping he had only partially burned, the one containing his likeness, was gone. He had the momentary exaltation of the artist who has captured the exact impression he sought.

Then he began to wonder if possibly he wasn't working too fast. As a means of creating the illusion that he was a badly wanted criminal the burning of the clippings was, he felt, a nice touch. Much more effective than displaying them intact. And the one that apparently had escaped both the fire and his attention would be enough to do the trick. But he was not at all sure that his prowler was Timothy Regan. If it were, if Regan himself had the clipping, he would know he could have demanded and got much more than the five hundred dollars he'd asked. But he hadn't done this. He hadn't raised the ante a nickel. Did this mean it hadn't been he who found the clipping? Or did it mean he was just nursing his victim along till the extent of Smith's resources was fully established?

Smith's second discovery was on his return to the bedroom. A vagrant breeze from the window stirred the warm air up close to the ceiling and Smith, being taller than most, caught a hint of fragrance that did not belong there; it was vague, ephemeral, but he could have sworn it was Black Narcissus. He was pleased with the thought that it had been the lovely Juanita rather than her old man who had been in the room. Not that he had any particular reason to love her, either. She it was who had started the bleeding process by tipping Regan *père* to Smith's vulnerability. Still, beauty was where you found it.

Sitting on the edge of the bed, he had removed one shoe and was thinking about the other when someone tapped briskly on the door. He dragged one of the pillows over the gun at his side. "Come in."

It was Juanita. She was now in black silk lounging pajamas and these did nothing to dispel his former impression that she was adequate, even luscious. Despite their blackness, they seemed to reflect light, to shimmer with her even breathing. Her hair was like polished mahogany, he decided. "Hello, baby." He began unlacing the other shoe. The odor of Black Narcissus was much stronger now, like heady wine in his nostrils.

She stood with her back to the door, eyes more gray than blue, lazily amused. "You're not exactly excited over my visit, are you?"

"I'm speechless."

She came and sat beside him on the bed. "Kiss me."

He kissed her. Their hands met on the gun under the pillow. She laughed throatily. "I must be losing the old appeal."

Smith transferred the gun to his other side. "You forget our first meeting, sweetheart. Besides, so few girls offer to kiss me that I always get just a little suspicious when they do." He smiled on her fondly. "A fine, confidence-inspiring wench you turned out to be."

She considered that. "Well, at least you didn't say 'bitch.' "

"That's for when I know you even better. Right now I'm being polite."

She looked at him. "What do you mean, even better?"

"You didn't have to sound off about me to your old man," he said accusingly. "You did, so as far as I'm concerned, that puts you in his class, a petty, chiseling racket with him on one end, the cops on the other, and guys like me in the middle."

"Pop is kind of petty, all right," she admitted.

"But you're not, I suppose!"

"No," she said, "I'm not. Pop is useful to me sometimes, so I let him have the crumbs from the table, but don't think I play for shirt-profits or half-grand passports." Quite suddenly she turned her eyes full on him, and now they were the color of slate and almost as opaque. "You talk big, McSweeney. How big are you?"

He tried hard not to overdo the start of surprise. Carefully careless, he let his hand drop on the gun. "Come again?"

"My God," she said, "couldn't you think of something better than 'Smith'?" She got up and moved over to the dresser and lit one of his cigarettes. Smoke from the first deep drag billowed from her lips. "That's what made me think you weren't worth fooling with, except for peanuts."

The gun was in his lap now. His long thin fingers caressed it. "What made you change your mind, baby?"

"I haven't—yet." She looked scornfully at the gun. "And you can quit trying to scare me with that, too. There're a couple guys out in the hall, a couple more below your window in the garden. You wouldn't get very far." She inhaled deeply, let smoke dribble out with her next words. "You're hot, McSweeney. So hot you're burning up. If I tell the local law who you really are, they'll send you back for the reward. If I tell the old man, he'll make you top the reward in return for a hide-out. You're between the well-known debbil and the sea, honey."

"Maybe," Smith said. "If I'm somebody named McSweeney. And if I don't decide to pop you off right now." He sighted along the gun at her girdle-less middle. "Your gorillas, if any, could hardly stop that, now could they?"

She sighed. "Let's quit horsing around. I told you before that I could go for you. Besides, we've each got something the other needs. We'd make a fine team."

"For how long?" Smith said. He shook his head. "I'm afraid I couldn't sleep comfortably with you in the same room, baby."

She laughed. "With me in the room you wouldn't want to sleep." She crushed out the cigarette, took a slow turn about the open space between door and window. Her body had the sensuous, feline grace of a tiger. "You did come over in a plane, didn't you?"

"Unh-unh. In a cab. It broke down and I had to walk."

She made an impatient gesture. "That may do for Captain Rodriguez Dolores Hernandez. It won't do for me. I told you I thought I heard a plane just before you came along. Later on I sent some of the help back to look. There were oil drippings and a plane's wheel marks in the sand."

"All right," Smith said amiably, "just for fun let's play I'm McSweeney and I came over in a plane." He breathed on his gun, polished the spot with the palm of a hand. "Then what?"

"The pilot a friend of yours?"

"Maybe."

She was definitely annoyed now. "Good God, do you have to go on playing coy? Either the guy's a friend of yours or you laid plenty of sugar on the line for that flight. In any case, he took a chance, and if he's willing to take one he'll take another."

Smith smiled at her. "Not only lovely, but a logician." He began cracking the knuckles of his left hand. "So I know a guy with a plane."

"I want him."

"But maybe he won't want you," Smith said. "He's kind of a funny guy. Now, if it was me—"

She struck at him as a snake strikes, swiftly and without warning. The back of her hand caught him across the mouth. But she was not swift enough to repeat, nor to get away from him. His hand pinioned her wrists. Rising, he forced them behind her and upward; his encircling arms held her body tight against his. "Little hell-cat," he said tenderly.

She went limp, her eyes lifted to meet his. "I'm sorry, McSweeney. I've got a hell of a temper."

"Sure you have, hon. Sure you have." He released her wrists but still held her close to him. One of his hands smoothed her hair, and presently he laid his mouth on hers. After a while he pushed her from him. "What's in it for this friend of mine—if I can get him? And what's in it for me?"

"Don't worry, you'll be taken care of."

"That's what I'm afraid of," Smith said. "After you're through with us we'll be taken care of."

"Don't be silly, lover. This is big stuff. It isn't just one little job. It goes on and on."

"Unless you get caught," he said. "Or don't you? Maybe it's just me and my friend that'll get caught, like—He narrowed his eyes at her. "What happened to your other boy?"

"What other boy?"

"Back in San Diego," he said easily, "there was talk of a mystery plane tangling with the border patrol."

Scorn twisted her mouth. "Those dopes! They don't know from up." She drew a deep breath, expelled it angrily. "No, this dimwit I had got drunk and dunked himself in the Pacific Ocean. The son of a bitch!"

He admired her elaborately. "One thing I like about you, baby, you don't waste your time on sentiment."

"Why should I?"

"No reason," he said. "I was just wondering if you'd mourn me when I'm gone, or if I'd rate the same epitaph he does." He watched her breasts rise and fall under the black silk. "By the way, who's the real boss around here—you or the old man?"

"I told you," she said. "I am. Regan takes what I choose

to let him have." Her eyes darted up to meet his for an instant. "Just the same, you'd better not mention what we've been talking about."

"Not me," Smith said. "I wouldn't tell that bastard anything." He decided he wouldn't, either, at least not for a while. It was interesting to know, though, that if necessary he might be able to play father against daughter, and vice versa. "Well, I'll see what I can do about a plane for you. I'm not promising anything."

"Try hard, darling. Mamma's counting on you." She held up her mouth. "Kiss me good-night?"

"Unh-unh." He gave her a small leer instead. "You've probably got a knife up your sleeve, all ready for the middle of my back." His shiver was not all pretense. Her utter callousness gave him goose pimples. "I can feel it there now."

"Playing hard to get, darling?"

He shook his head. "Just not rolling over yet." He began to unbutton his shirt. "Tell you what I will do, though. For a bottle of Scotch tonight I'll kiss you twice in the morning."

"It's a deal," she said. "I'll send up a boy." As she opened the door he saw that she hadn't been lying about the two men in the hall. They were really there.

Chapter 14

By the light of day Captain Rodriguez Dolores Hernandez looked slightly less handsome and debonair than he had the night before. He looked as though he had not slept well. There were bags under his eyes, his mustache was not so crisply pointed and his brown skin had a faint yellowish cast. He regarded Smith with sullen, unfriendly eyes. "You say you 'ave come over from Tijuana?"

Smith nodded. The forget permit furnished him by Regan lay on the captain's desk, but for some reason Hernandez was not reacting to it as he should. Outside the door, in the main office of the *cárcel,* a couple of telegraph keys clacked noisily and there was the drone of many voices. Unlike most of the jails Smith had been in, this one appeared busier by day than at night.

Hernandez drummed carefully manicured fingers on the desk. "It is strange we do not find the taxicab you say brings you. We 'ave communicate with Tijuana."

Smith was indignant. "So what? Maybe he hasn't got back there yet. Maybe he stopped over to visit relatives on the way." He thumped the desk. "Is that permit any good or isn't it?"

Hernandez looked at his nails, at a pile of letters. He looked out the window. He looked everywhere except directly as Smith. "What is your interest in the Señorita Regan?"

"I told you," Smith said. "I helped her change a tire and she gave me a lift into town."

"And later she 'ave visit you in your room," Hernandez said. He was not guessing. He was stating a fact, although one that obviously did not give him any happiness.

Smith struggled with the impulse to run, to get the hell out of there. There were just too many wheels within wheels around here, too many people with eyes in the backs of their heads. Juanita Regan had had two of her own men outside Smith's door; she had claimed to have two more stationed in the garden below his window. Surely Hernandez or one of his spies couldn't have got close enough to see what had actually transpired in the room. And it was not likely that Juanita herself would have mentioned it. Yet here was Hernandez, right on the ball with all the latest dope. Smith managed a nonchalant shrug. "The lady had recommended the hotel to me. She wished merely to assure herself of my comfort."

Hernandez was not entirely convinced. He gave every evidence of being a jealous lover who for the moment lacks sufficient proof of the loved one's infidelity to precipitate action. He stood up. "This is Mexico, señor. Except for *el jefe* I am in supreme authority in Los Gatos. If I find that you 'ave lie to me—"

"Listen," Smith said earnestly, "from now on I won't even let the maid in to make up my bed."

"You will please to stay away from the Señorita Regan."

"I will," Smith promised. "Cross my heart." He wondered if perhaps *el capitán* wasn't an honest man; if in spite of the permit squeeze he was knowingly a party to it, or to the lovely Juanita's *sub rosa* activities. He turned toward the door, paused. "I suppose the Regans are now citizens of Mexico?"

It appeared they were not. They were still of the Estados Unidos, a fact that seemed to add to the captain's gloom. "I bid you good day, Señor Smith. *Adios.*"

"*Adios,*" Smith said. He went out.

Along the Avenida Juan Batista the little shops and tourist traps were coming alive. Under the wooden canopies shading sidewalks and store fronts from a blazing sun were piled high all the usual and incredibly ugly items calculated to attract the naïve visitor from above the border: misshapen ollas, gaudy serapes, strings of brightly painted gourds, stacks of straw sombreros, mountains of more or less authentic Indian baskets. Inside the windows and on tables beyond wide-flung doors, copper and silver filigree kept company with ropes of beads, pictures of the Virgin Mary, and the inexhaustible, omnipresent piles of Mexican cigarettes.

Smith found all this activity, this scurry and bustle, a little sad, here in Los Gatos, for he knew, as did the merchants themselves, that there were not and probably would never be again enough customers to go around. Few tourists would brave the seventy miles of bad road for the same stuff they could buy right in Tia Juana. There was even talk of discontinuing the daily boat from San Diego, a cruise that used to pack them in when there was prohibition in the United States and legal gambling in Mexico. Los Gatos was slowly starving to death and making a brave effort to conceal the fact beneath a cloak of gaiety.

Not that there weren't plenty of people in evidence, but the brown ones weren't interested in gewgaws, and the few whites were not the sucker type. Down toward the wharf, in the middle of the small plaza, a band was tuning up against the arrival of the unwary gringo, but as yet there was no sign of the ship itself. There were not so many boats at anchor as there had been the night before. Two soldiers with rifles stood at attention outside the customs shed. The whole scene had the artificial look of a movie set just readied for the day's shooting.

The only establishment not alive to the imminent Yankee dollar was that of Jesus Ortega. The tobacco and periodical shop was still closed. Apparently its proprietor was either a very late sleeper or just didn't give a damn. About the time Smith satisfied himself of this he discovered that he was being tailed. It was a definite feeling, like waking in the night and knowing someone is in your room. He crossed the street and entered the haberdashery next door to Ortega's place. The haberdasher was glad to see him. He would have been glad to see anybody with money to spend. Selecting shirts and socks and shorts, Smith kept one eye on the sidewalk he had just quitted and presently identified his shadow, a rather too ostentatious loiterer before a *botica* window in which there was nothing but dried herbs. The man was one of the two Juanita Regan had posted in the hall outside Smith's room as her personal insurance of health. The lady, it seemed, was nothing if not thorough.

Smith paid for his purchases, accepting a brown paper-wrapped bundle. "What's the matter with the guy next door?"

"Ortega?" the proprietor shrugged. "Sometimes he goes away, stays two, three days."

"Fishing, perhaps?"

The man's smile became somewhat less genial. "I do not know, señor. Ortega, he is not tell me these things."

"Well, I'm glad to see there's somebody in town who doesn't need money," Smith said pleasantly, and took his departure. As he stepped to the sidewalk he observed that there was someone else interested in Ortega. A small dapper man with the look of a race-track tout was rattling the latch of Ortega's door and muttering to himself with a kind of frustrated rage. He was Cagy, the peddler of pornography and alleged dealer in certain powders. "The son of a bitch," he said. He saw Smith. "Hi, pally."

"Hi."

Active suspicion sharpened the little man's face. "You ain't been shopping around, have you, pally?"

"Only for a clean shirt," Smith said, deciding that there was something even funnier about the missing Mr. Ortega than he had at first thought. "Why don't you kick the goddam door down?" he suggested. "Maybe teach him a lesson." He recrossed the street, so that his waiting shadow wouldn't be inconvenienced. He felt that it would be nice if the man could report to his mistress that he, Smith, had used a telephone. He had no intention of contacting anyone, at least not yet, about the airplane the lady wanted, but it would be well to say that he had tried.

He had just spotted a Mexican National telephone sign outside the Oro Grande Hotel when he heard his name called. "Reed! Reed Smith, wait a minute!" It was a feminine voice, and melodious enough, but at the moment it was the last voice in the world he wanted to hear. Somehow, God only knew by what freak of circumstance, Miss Linda Van Owen was in Los Gatos and practically breathing down his neck. Cursing soundlessly but fervently, he pretended he was stone-deaf and lenghtened his stride, hoping to make the sanctuary of the Oro Grande before she actually caught up with him.

He was unsuccessful. Halfway up the hotel steps he felt her hand on his arm. "Reed, please!"

Not looking at her, he spoke from a corner of his mouth. "Get away from me."

"No, I—"

"Good Christ!" He was aware of the swart, greasy man

who was tailing him, so close he could almost smell the garlic-laden breath. Turning, he saw a paunchy Mexican cop ambling toward them along the sidewalk. He thrust Linda hard against the swart man, yanked her violently away, making it appear that the swart man had pushed her. "Who the hell you think you're shoving, greaseball?"

Greaseball was astonished. "Señor, I do not—" His shrug, his spread hands, were meant to indicate denial, apology if necessary, but Smith chose to interpret the gesture as a threat. He hit the swart man smack on the chin, watched him fall, saw the inevitable crowd gathering, and pushed Linda ahead of him into the lobby. Momentarily they were alone.

"Well!" Linda said, and again: "Well!" She was a little out of breath. "What was the meaning of all that?"

"Listen," Smith said, and gripped her arm hard enough to make her wince. "Whatever you're doing down here, I don't want any part of it. I'm working." He released her. "Now get away from me and stay away."

"Don't you suppose I know you're working?" She rubbed her arm. "El Guadalupe will know it too if he sees you."

He was incredulous. "Lupe—down here?" He tried to look at her and the front door at the same time. "In Los Gatos?"

She nodded. "I just followed him over from Tia Juana." Her voice grew bitter. "I thought you'd appreciate being warned to look out for him."

He felt little icy prickles of apprehension along his spine. "Then this isn't an accident? You knew I was here?" He saw the paunchy cop coming up the steps. "How?"

She stamped her foot impatiently. "If you must know, it was Cassidy, damn it. I—" She broke off as a second cop joined the first and together they came through the door.

The fat one was panting a little. Between puffs he explained to his companion that this man here, this tall man, was the one who had struck Pablo down. He himself had seen it. He addressed Smith. "For why you do this thing, señor?"

Smith was indignant. "Did you not see him push this lady?" He bent a solicitous gaze on Linda. "You are unharmed, madam? You are recovered from your fright?"

"Oh, quite," she assured him dryly. She gave the two constables a radiant smile. "Really, it was nothing. The man is probably drunk. I shall not prefer charges against him."

They looked relieved. They put their heads close together,

conferring. The fat one spoke to Smith. "You are acquaint with the lady, señor?"

Smith said no, he wasn't; that he had never seen her before, but gallantly added that this was his loss. "If I didn't have a business appointment I'd like nothing better than to buy the lady a drink. He lifted his hat, bowed to Linda, to the constables, and hurried out. Inwardly he was seething, this time his rage directed at Cassidy. He was also more than a little frightened, for if El Guadalupe chanced to be visiting the Regans, as now seemed quite possible, then a meeting and instant recognition were almost inevitable. He entered the express office, bought change, and sought a phone booth, where he attempted to reach Cassidy at a private number in San Diego. There was no answer. Emerging into the sunlight again, the first person he saw was Cassidy.

For an undercover operation this was certainly turning into a three-ring circus. He was impelled to leap on Cassidy and murder him right there, but habit was strong within him. He turned away, began walking rapidly up the sreet.

"Hey, you!" Cassidy yelled. "You with the long legs!"

Smith stretched his walk to a run. People on the sidewalk made room for him, stopped to stare as he went by. Behind him Cassidy's voice rose to a bellow. "Hey, McSweeney!" There was a shot.

Smith stumbled, went to his knees. He was not hit; he merely pretended to be; to struggle to his feet again even as Cassidy, noisily triumphant, fell on his back. Together they rolled into the gutter, wrestling furiously. "She tricked me!" Cassidy panted. "So help me God, I never saw a woman could drink like that one!"

"You son of a bitch," Smith grunted, whamming a fist into Cassidy's belly. "She couldn't have got you drunk if you hadn't been trying to beat my time."

Around them a fast-gathering crowd cheered impartially as first one, then the other got the upper hand. Cassidy's breathing was quite audible now, realistic as hell. "She was just so goddam worried about you, so she said, and maybe I was too, and then when I woke up this morning and remembered, I got really worried." He let Smith beat his head on the pavement. "She gum the works?"

Smith's teeth were bared, his face vicious. "You and her both. Get her out of here." It was now his turn to be on the bottom. Cassidy struck with the gun, miscalculated a trifle, and almost sheared an ear off. "Cops coming," Smith panted. He seized the gun, fired. Cassidy collapsed. Smith hauled himself erect, menaced the crowd. "Don't anybody move!" He picked up his bundle and ran.

Chapter 15

"This is going to cost you dough," Regan said. He faced Smith in a dim corridor of the hotel's closed wing. Though it was broad daylight outside, there was no evidence of it in here. A window at the far end was boarded up with a sheet of plywood. A low-wattage bulb burned yellowly against the ceiling, casting their shadows, one long and thin, the other squat and misshapen, on thick carpeting that smelled a little musty. "How much dough you got, sucker?"

"Enough."

"This guy you think you may have killed—he a copper?"

"A Fed," Smith said.

Regan shook his head. "Jesus, you pick on the damnedest people. The first guy you socked—Pablo—is Captain Hernandez's brother."

Smith thought that this was interesting. Not only because it explained how Hernandez had known of Juanita's visit to Smith's room last night, but because Pablo seemed capable of working for two bosses at once. It was also further evidence, had he needed it, that news traveled very fast in Los Gatos. He himself was still short of breath from running. "That shouldn't worry you, not with your drag."

Regan shrugged. "Maybe, maybe not." His eyes glittered. "How much dough you say you had?"

"I didn't say."

Regan's grin was again reminiscent of Grandma's stand-in. "I don't just got to hide you out, sucker. It's your neck, not mine."

"You're already into me for half a grand," Smith protested.

"You got what you paid for," Regan said. "It's not my fault if you washed it down the sewer."

"All right," Smith said grudgingly, "I'll go another five hundred. That's for now. Maybe there'll be more later, when and if I get squared." He saw cupidity leap in Regan's eyes. "But don't get any cute ideas. The really big stuff isn't on me."

"Who, me?" Regan wore an injured air. "When I make a deal it's a deal." After a moment he said: "Okay, I'll take you on, but, brother, you're plenty hot and I'm giving you a bargain." He started down the corridor, halted. "I'll have to have your gun."

"No."

Regan thrust out his jaw. "Listen, brother, it's a rule of the house: you shed your gun or you don't come in. I can't take the chance of one of you muggs popping a cannon." He shook his head stubbornly. "No rod, no dice."

Smith hesitated, finally produced the gun he had taken away from Cassidy. His own remained comfortably warm and snug in the waistband of his trousers. "I don't like this," he said worriedly. "I don't like it a little bit."

"You'll be all right," Regan assured him, and pocketed the weapon. "You have any arguments with the rest of the boys, use your fists." He led the way around an ell in the corridor. "Or your feet, for all I care." He unlocked a big solid-looking door and they went through it into an enormous chamber that had originally been designed as a ballroom. There still were patches of unscarred dance floor. A series of tall windows, once draped with an eye to symmetrical effect, was now blanked out with a careless hodgepodge of oil paintings, oriental rugs, old blankets, and, in one place, a tapestry depicting the *Last Supper*. From previous observation Smith knew that the windows were not only covered within; they were boarded up on the outside too. The general idea seemed to be to keep out all possible air and sunlight. The few unbroken bulbs in the ornate ceiling chandeliers glowed yellow and sickly through a fog of cigarette smoke, giving the whole scene an air of unreality, like something pictured in a Fu Manchu opus. There were between twenty and thirty men in the room. Curiously, there was very little noise.

Against the far wall was a row of double-tiered bunks, many of them rumpled and unkempt as the men themselves. A bar knocked together out of planks and barrels; half a dozen baize-covered tables; a nondescript assortment of chairs made up the bulk of the furniture. Smith estimated that the rewards on half the men in sight would total well over a hundred thousand dollars. Of the rest, those not easily recognizable from their broadcast pictures, many had an unmistakably foreign look. Europeans, probably, on their way into the United States, rather than fleeing from it. There were four or five Chinese. Eyes lifted from cards, newspapers, or morose contemplation of nothing at all to examine Smith briefly, then dropped away as if he were without interest.

Regan piloted him to the bar. "The first one is on me," he said. "After that they're a dollar a throw."

Smith accepted this information without enthusiasm. "You must make a nice thing out of it, pappy." He sipped his Scotch, was surprised to find it good. "What do you do when they run out of money—cut their throats?"

"They either find some more money or they scram the hell out of here," Regan said. "This ain't a charitable institution."

Smith laughed. "By God, I'm beginning to like you. Your daughter too. You don't pretend to be something you're not. A guy knows where he stands. "He lowered his voice. "You mean you just kick 'em out on their fannies?"

"I ain't the U.S. government," Regan said. "I ain't the mint."

"I didn't mean that." Smith tossed off the rest of his drink. "It strikes me you're missing an angle, that's all. If I were running a clip joint like this, and had an in with the local law, I'd see the cops were tipped off when I was about to spring a member for nonpayment of dues."

Regan put his glass down slowly. "Now there's an idea, ain't it?" He regarded Smith with something akin to admiration. "You know, sucker, you're smarter than I gave you credit for."

"Of course," Smith pointed out, "if word got around among the boys back home, they might be a little sore."

"Hell with that." Regan's mind was chewing the cud of Smith's suggestion and linking it. "I'm running a business."

"Sure you are," Smith. His leer would have made a satyr envious. "You or your daughter, one."

Anger showed briefly in Regan's cold eyes. His undershot jaw became even more pronounced. "Come again?"

"There seems to be a difference of opinion around here as to who's really the big wheel. I just thought I'd find out before I commit myself to anything."

Regan's hairy fist closed on Smith's arm. "What's she up to now?"

"If she were my daughter I might ask her," Smith said. Turning away he paused to add: "But if you do, leave me out of it. I don't want any part of a family squabble." He crossed the room and picked out a chair and a tattered magazine. When presently he looked up from an advertisement offering to send him a truss by mail in a plain wrapper he saw Regan climbing the grand staircase; saw him unlock a pair of heavy bronze doors, like those in a theater lobby, and go through, no doubt locking them behind him again.

He wondered what these twenty- or thirty-odd men thought they were getting out of such an existence. They were little better than prisoners, and they were certainly paying through the nose for what protection they got. He thought that personally he would rather take the rap and have it over with. Unless, of course, it happened to be a murder rap. He began a story about a young heiress who wanted to be loved for herself alone, so she took a job in Woolworth's. It was the same story he'd been trying to read for years, only sometimes the job was in a shoe factory or a department store.

A burly man with a badly set broken nose got up from a stud game and came over to sit in the chair beside Smith's. He spoke from one side of his mouth. "Come south for your health?"

"That was the original idea," Smith said. "Now I'm not so sure." He looked with obvious distaste at his surroundings. "Why do you guys stand for it?"

"Oh, it ain't so bad. They feed good here, and anyway, when the heat cools a little, I'm shoving back over the right side of the line."

Smith's mouth twisted into a sneer. "That's if this bastard Regan sees fit to tell you when the heat's off."

The burly man let the front legs of his chair down slowly, deliberately. "What's on your mind, chum?"

"Nothing," Smith said, "except that I hear he's a two-timing son of a bitch." His gaze touched his companion's face briefly. "A guy like that could milk you dry and then spring you right into the middle of some waiting law."

"You don't really think that, do you, chum?"

"I'm kicking it around," Smith said. "He doesn't look to me like a guy who'd pass up the chance to cut in on a reward."

"Well, by Jesus!" the burly man said. Then he said, as though trying to convince himself rather than Smith: "No, he wouldn't dare!"

Smith felt that he had scattered enough trouble seeds for a while. He yawned widely. "Probably not," he agreed. "It was just a thought." He closed his eyes, pretending to sleep. For what seemed a like a long time he could feel the man's hard unwinking stare on his face, could feel himself being measured, weighed. Then presently he knew that he was alone, though in leaving the man had made no sound.

With his eyes shut, he listened to the various noises in the great room. in addition to the stud game, somebody had started shooting craps, and there was an argument about whether they treated you better at San Quentin than they did at Folsom. A heavy German accent was discussing with an even thicker Italian accent the merits of Argentina as against those of the United States. They settled for the States, mainly for fiscal reasons, Smith gathered.

He discovered that only half his mind was engaged with this game. The other half was on Linda. What had she been doing in Tia Juana, that she would be in a position to follow Lupe down here? He remembered the unresolved debate over her gun, and it occurred to him now that she was exactly the type of young lady who would go to El Guadalupe and demand its return. He hoped Cassidy would have to use force, getting her out of Los Gatos. He wouldn't mind adminstering a little discipline himself, for though her information was of some value, her own presence was almost as inimical to his project as Lupe's.

Incidentally, where was the effeminate but dangerous fat man now? Was he filling the lovely Juanita's ear with tidings of a man named Smith and a girl named Linda Van Owen?

Or if by chance Lupe and Miss Regan were unacquainted, could not the man Pablo do as good a job? On the whole, though, Smith felt that he could discredit Pablo's tidings easier than he could El Guadalupe's. He felt that Pablo's own position was somewhat equivocal.

Deciding presently that his morale needed bolstering, he borrowed a razor and carried it and his bundle of fresh linen into the adjoining washroom. When he emerged some little time later he was clean, refreshed, presentable. Aware of an unusual stillness in the room, he thought at first that he himself was the cause. Then he turned and saw Juanita Regan on the stairs, motionless, surveying the scene below her with a kind of royal disdain. She was wearing a white sports suit and from where he stood he had an excellent view of a pair of legs without flaw. He looked at the upturned faces of his fellow inmates. Their eyes, their mouths, were animal: celibacy had sharpened their appetites. He thought that the least sign of fear on her part would precipitate a riot. He was apprehensive when her gaze settled on him and she crooked a beckoning finger. He wished she had singled out someone else for her favor. As he went toward her he could feel, like knives at his back, the hate and greed and envy of the others.

When he was still a few steps below her he saw that the pupils of her eyes were abnormally large and almost black, and he was suddenly a little sorry for her, though no less watchful. He had no means of knowing whether she was a confirmed addict or had just had herself a shot as a temporary expedient, but in any case she was as unpredictable, as loaded with unpleasant potentialities, as an unexploded mine.

"I've a good mind to toss you to those wolves down there," she said viciously. "If I told them to they'd tear you apart."

"I believe you, darling." He offered her an ingratiating smile. "And I really am sorry about this morning, but it wasn't a total bust. I did phone my friend about the plane."

"You did? What did he say?"

"He's interested."

She hesitated a moment, eyes bright and hard and probing. "All right, let's go upstairs." She turned and led the way.

The apartment they came to was done in white and gold, with only here and there a splash of bright color to give it warmth. Heavy white velour drapes were drawn over windows presumably boarded up, but the air was fresh, faintly perfumed. Light came from crystal wall brackets and from a shaded reading lamp beside a white-and-gold damask chaise longue. There was an open magazine turned face-down on the chaise and he had an almost hysterical impulse to laugh when he saw that its title was *House & Garden*.

She sat at one end of an outsize divan, kicked off her pumps, and tucked her feet under her. The homey act, the magazine, the atmosphere of the room nearly lured him into a sense of security. Then he raised admiring eyes from her knees and saw that she was holding a pistol in her lap. She held it loosely but competently, its muzzle directed at his stomach. He sighed. "That again!"

A brief tremor shook her body. Her voice was tight, as though controlled with difficulty. "Listen, McSweeney, I just shot one man. I can make it two." And when he said nothing to that: "You don't believe me?" The hand and pistol made a small imperative gesture. "Take a look under that throw rug."

There were three excellent reasons for humoring her: she was a woman; she had a skinful of hop; she had a gun in her fist. With the toe of his right shoe he lifted an edge of the white shag rug and saw on the carpet beneath it a spreading scarlet stain, which presently would turn brown. He covered it over again. "Anybody I know, baby?"

She laughed, a brittle sound that had a hint of triumph in it. "What ever gave you that idea?"

"I thought it might be Pablo," he said mildly. "He's been carrying tales to his brother about you being in my room last night." He shook his head at her, smiling. "Hernandez suggested that I keep away from you."

She stirred a little, but her eyes did not leave his face. "Let's talk about the girl, McSweeney. Who was she?"

"Not till you stop waving guns at me," he said. He no longer smiled. "I'm not one of those stir-happy bums you've got caged up downstairs."

"Aren't you forgetting the spot you're in?"

"I've got out of worse."

"Have you, now?" The faintest of Irish brogues colored the three words. Even white teeth glistened between parted red lips. She lifted the pistol and fired.

Something tugged at his coat where it lay against his hip, little more than the flick of an impatient hand. Gun sound racketed around the room for an instant, was muffled, absorbed by hangings, carpet, upholstery. He did not move.

Her eyes were wide, incredulous. "You knew I didn't mean to hit you?"

"If I'd thought you did I'd have shot you first, precious." He let her see the wide butt of the weapon in his waistband then. "Don't think I wouldn't, or couldn't have."

Her sudden pallor was of rage, not fear. "That God-damned Regan!" She stood up, the pistol falling unheeded to the floor. "I can't depend on him for anything any more!"

"Poppa was a little careless in this instance," Smith admitted. He bent and picked up her gun, considered it thoughtfully for a moment, finally tossed it on the chaise, where it made a rather unique decorative note beside *House & Garden.* In the down-filled cushion at the chaise's head he saw a neat round hole that might easily have been in him had not the lady been such a remarkably good shot. He was grateful to whoever had taught her. "While we're on the subject of brains," he said, "you haven't exhibited an over-supply yourself. Who's this guy you claim you shot?"

"You wouldn't know him," she said. She put on her shoes, straightened to regard him searchingly. "At least I don't think you would." The telephone rang and she went to it quickly. "Yes? Yes? . . . You didn't get anything out of him first?" Sudden fury contorted her face. "The God-damned fairy!" She hurled the instrument from her, snatched it up, banged it into its cradle. "Oh, damn him, damn him!" She saw Smith watching her, flushed, bit her lip, abruptly began to laugh. "I'm not a very nice person, am I, darling?"

"Well," Smith said carefully, "a man would never get bored around you, anyway." He did not know why she had done it, but he would have given odds that the man she had shot was El Guadalupe, and that the fat, effeminate one, impervious to her charms in life, was now even beyond the more brutal persuasion of her thugs. He was torn between relief and a desire to go some place and be sick at his stomach.

"I do hate to be beaten," she said. "Especially by a—" She frowned. "Well, never mind that now." She came to him, put her arms around him, her body flat against his. "Tell me about the girl, darling?"

"There's nothing to that. She's a society fair that likes to play around in gutters. I met her in a hide-out in San Diego."

She was not entirely satisfied. "You put on quite an act with her and Pablo."

He pushed her away from him. "I don't like people tailing me, baby. Not even yours." He laughed. "At the time, I didn't know he was Hernandez's brother. He was just a guy who had his nose and ears where they had no business to be. He made me nervous."

"And the other one, the Federal dick—did he make you nervous too?"

"Nervous! Coming right on top of the run-in with the girl he damn' near scared the pants off me." He lit a cigarette, snapped the match at a bowl of red-bronze chrysanthemums. "He's one of the guys that chased me the hell out of El Paso and Juarez."

"You don't think she led him to you?"

He looked at her. "By God, I hadn't thought of that." He appeared to consider the possibility for a moment, finally shook his head. "No, she couldn't have. He may have been tailing her on another angle, but— What happened to them, anyway?"

"The last I heard, they were still with Hernandez. His cops are looking all over hell and gone for you." She took the cigarette from him, inhaled deeply, blew twin streams of smoke from her nostrils. "All right, let's talk about the plane, shall we? When can I get in?"

"There you go," he complained. "Always interested in what you get, not what anybody else gets."

She stood on tiptoe, put her mouth on his. "Don't you like me, darling?"

"That's neither here nor there," he said stubbornly. "Even at war-surplus prices this friend of mine has got six or seven thousand dollars tied up in that crate. He's got his neck to think of. I've got mine. We want to know what's in it to make us risk all that."

She released him, let her arms fall to her sides. "I'll bet

you never kissed your own mother without a guaranteed profit in sight."

"Look who's talking!" He lit another cigarette, laughed smoke out of his mouth. "What's the deal—smuggling those Chinks and other aliens over the line?"

"You don't like that?"

"No," he said, "and I'll tell you why. They're took bulky: this plane could handle only three or four at a time, five at most. Say you get a grand a head. Split three ways, four if you include your old man—" He shrugged. "There's not enough in it for the gamble."

"I've been doing all right."

He showed her a smile that held little or no merriment. "Sure. You collect in advance and sit on your cute little bottom while the other guy takes the risks. If I remember right, your last pilot took one too many. He's dead."

She laughed at him. "Well?"

With some difficulty he mastered the impulse to take her lovely neck in his two hands and crack it. "All right, say they're expendable. That can go on for just so long, then you're in trouble. Matter of fact, you're in trouble right now. That's why you're dickering with me."

"You know that isn't true." Her eyes, her voice were reproachful. "Oh, darling, can't you see that—I've waited so long for someone I could trust—really trust—"

"Stop it," he said. "I know how much you trust me. Less than ten minutes ago you were flourishing a gun and bragging about this one and that one you'd killed."

"But that was before—" She looked at him from beneath lowered lids. "Suppose I told you that now, as of this afternoon, I've got hold of something really big. I've got it all to my own sweet self. We can forget Regan, forget those nasty Chinese and Hunyaks you don't like." Excited color came into her cheeks, her eyes were brilliant. "Nobody but you and Juanita, pet. What do you say?"

He pretended to be only half convinced. "This isn't just the dope in you talking? It's on the level?"

"Come on, I'll show you." She ran laughing into the bedroom. Following more slowly, he saw her wrestling a heavy pigskin bag from among other luggage on a closet floor. It was not much larger than an overnight case, but lifting it to the broad Hollywood bed left her a little breathless. She unlocked and flung the lid with the air of a magician producing rabbits from a hat. "There! Fifty grand right here in Mexico, darling. Twice that in California, wholesale."

The bag was packed solid with tins of varying shapes and

sizes. Some of them still bore the original labels of drug firms in as widely separated places as Holland, Malaya, Brazil. With his penknife he broke the seal on one, saw what looked like cocaine crystals. A moistened finger carried a minute portion of the substance to his tongue. It was cocaine. He replaced the lid, looked at her admiringly. "This is more like it, precious. You've bought yourself a man." He put an arm around her waist. "Who's your contact in the States?"

For a moment he was afraid he had gone too fast, had betrayed himself. She twisted free of him, her face pale with fury, a torrent of blasphemy rushing from her lips. Then he realized that none of it was directed at him, but at the man who had outsmarted her by dying before he could be made to talk. "But I'll find out," she told him presently. "Don't think I won't."

"Sure you will." His voice was tender, soothing. "Sure you will, baby." He was almost as furious as she at this sudden dead end, but at least he had made, was making, definite progress. He considered probing for her source of supply, decided not to press his luck.

Some of her former gaiety had returned. "This is only the beginning, darling." Her eyes, her hands caressed the contents of the pigskin case. "It goes on and on, forever and ever and ever."

"Amen." He took a slow turn about the room, paused before an elaborate dressing-table littered with more than the usual quota of expensive items. Among them was a framed snapshot of a man standing beside a ricksha against a background that could have been Shanghai or Singapore. He looked as though he might develop into an Old China Hand if he stayed there long enough; as though he would know all about polo ponies and rugger and maybe cricket. He was Chris Lancaster.

Chapter 16

As the afternoon wore on into evening he was aware of a mounting tension in the great room which had once echoed to music and laughter and dancing feet. The men were sullen, disinclined to talk, except on those occasions when three or four of them would abruptly go into a huddle apart from their fellows. Though he was not pointedly ostracized, neither was he invited to join these various groups, and at first he ascribed this to the fact that he was a newcomer and thus more or less on trial before being admitted to the fraternity. Then it occurred to him that it was because he, rather than one of the initiate, who had been selected as the queen's consort for a matter of two hours or so. He wished they knew how really little reason they had to be jealous.

Regan had been in twice since Smith's return from the bridal suite, but at neither time had he approached Smith or any of the others, rather self-consciously, it seemed, ignoring them in favor of his satellite the bartender, a brutish man with almost no forehead and a drooping mustache reminiscent of the John L. Sullivan era. Regan appeared to have something on his mind, a preoccupation with something outside the ballroom, which tended to make him insensible to the restlessness of his charges. Smith, who had considerable on his own mind, was nevertheless able to detect a tightening up among the men when Regan was present; it was as though their individual disaffections and hatreds became merged and focused on the squat, unlovely figure of their host. He hoped that the small seed of trouble he had planted earlier was not going to bear fruit till after his own project had matured. Flat on his back in one of the unused bunks, he momentarily experienced the feeling of being trapped, of trying to function in a vacuum. The rest of the cast were outside, free to roam the wipe-open spaces, to ad-lib action and dialogue as they saw fit, while he, who should have been the leading man, was confined within these four walls, not only physically but by circumstances over which he now had no control.

Presumably a plane would arrive that night, piloted by the same Jerry who had made the first trip. But unfortunately Smith had had to arrange for it under the watchful eye of Miss Juanita Regan, a terrific handicap, for with her sitting right there beside him the telephonic conversation was necessarily limited. He would have preferred a nice private booth somewhere outside, but at the time this was manifestly impossible. Even escaping her vigilance, he couldn't have gone wandering around town in broad daylight. Every cop in Mexico was alerted for him and probably ordered to shoot on sight.

He wished he knew more about the Hernandez-Regan set-up. If Hernandez was an honest cop, how could the Regans have been using him, and his brother Pablo, as certain of the evidence seemed to indicate? On the other hand, if he was crooked, why the need for all the elaborate secrecy involving this room and its occupants?

He considered the probability that George Falconer was Juanita's San Diego connection. Almost certainly he had been Lupe's. But apparently she hadn't known that, though she may since have found out. Or the whole business could have been merely an act for Smith's benefit. He turned his theory over in his mind, discarding it presently on the grounds that if for one instant she had doubted his authenticity she could have had him knocked off long before this.

Well, he'd just have to play the cards as they fell and leave it up to the boys on the receiving end to seize opportunity by the forelock. He had no idea whether she intended to accompany the first load herself, whether he would, or they both would. He had no idea where Chris Lancaster fitted into the scheme of things. The man's picture on her dressing-table, apparently treasured for some years, since Lancaster was obviously older now, suggested a former intimacy; indeed, a depth of feeling entirely out of keeping with the lady's character as he knew it. But say that she was capable of the great emotion, that it was reciprocated, that she and Lancaster were in alliance, she on the one end, he on the other. Where did that put George Falconer, and why was she thrown for a loss by the too sudden death of El Guadalupe? It was too bad that Smith couldn't have asked her to clarify a few of these matters for him. That well-worn cliché about the lap of the gods occurred to him, and after a fruitless search for a better one, he let it ride. He decided that even had his talk with Cassidy not been hampered by Juanita's presence he wouldn't have been believed anyway. Nobody, not even the gray man, would believe what a beautiful, luscious, utterly ruthless bitch she was.

His meditations were interrupted by a mellow, sonorous voice at his elbow. "Asleep, pilgrim?"

He opened his eyes and saw standing beside the bunk a man even taller and thinner than himself, a man dressed in sober black who had the look of a small-town clergyman. "No," he said. "Just thinking."

"About friend Regan, perhaps?"

"Maybe," Smith assented cautiously, and struggled to a sitting position. Lank black hair and deep-set dark eyes gave his visitor's face a Lincolnesque quality. Quite suddenly he recognized the man as a celebrated wife-murderer, a regular modern-day Bluebeard. "What's on your mind?"

"Many things, pilgrim, many things." He cleared his throat gently. "But uppermost in our good boniface, Timothy Regan. It is your considered opinion that he would sell us out at a price?"

Smith earnestly wished that he had kept his mouth shut when approached by the burly man with the cauliflower ear and broken nose. At the time it had seemed like a good idea;

he could not possibly have foreseen the curious chain of events that had since taken place. But that was of no help now. He phrased his reply with some care. "Don't let anything I said influence you."

Some subtle change took place in the man's face, in the timbre of his voice. Both were slightly less benevolent. "You have revised your opinion? You now feel that he is to be trusted?"

"Not at all," Smith said. His mouth felt parched, the palms of his hands moist and sticky. If he had needed one more thing to make his position completely insecure, this was it. He had been maneuvered into a spot where he must definitely align himself with the wolves so avidly watching him, or with Regan. He tossed Regan overboard. "Trust that bastard? Not me!"

"Thank you, pilgrim." The mellow-voiced, ministerial wife-murderer went away. Smith held his breath for all of ten seconds; he surreptitiously wiped his sweaty palms along the seams of his trousers; he got to his feet and by a roundabout route, being very careful not to run, he approached the bar, where he ordered and drank three double Scotches, one right after another. He began to feel better. After a while he felt almost invincible.

At seven o'clock dinner was brought in and served by two slattern Indian women, bulky in many skirts, earthy-smelling, giggling at the ribald remarks and obscene gestures of the men. But the food was plentiful and good. Smith ate with the greedy abandon and disregard for Emily Post as his companions in crime. He had not realized how hungry he was, how utterly famished. He decided that it was his empty stomach that had been making him so jumpy. Presently, replete, he repaired to his bunk to conserve his strength against his hour of need. He felt that in the matter of Juanita Regan, the clandestine arrival of an airplane and some hundred-odd thousands of dollars in heroin, cocaine, and morphine, strength would be necessary, not to say a modicum of sagacity and tact. He hoped he would be equal to the task. He decided he would direct his keen, machine-like mind to the problem and no doubt solve it handily. But after a time he grew a little tired and somewhat discouraged and finally gave it up. There were too many unknown factors. He could not think of a suitable substitute for the lap-of-the-gods cliché, either.

The bruiser with the cauliflower ear and badly set nose came over. "How'd you make out with her nibs this afternoon, pally?"

"All right."

"Jesus, you ain't very enthusiastic. How was she?"

"I'm a gentleman," Smith said.

"Yes, you are!"

"And anyway," Smith said, "don't get the idea that it's for free." He shook his head sadly. "Nothing's for free around here."

"You said it." Under brows thick with scar tissue the man's eyes were sharp with interest. "What've you got that I ain't?"

Smith felt that a salting of truth might lend veracity to such lies as became necessary. "She thinks I know where there's a plane." He jerked a thumb at the five Chinese huddled to themselves in a far corner. "The last guy she had to run them got knocked off."

"She got any reason for thinkin' that, pally?"

"Maybe."

The bury man sighed. "And me without hardly an airplane to my name." He unwrapped and folded a stick of gum, popped it into his mouth, slowly masticated. "Some of the boys been talkin' things over. What with this and that, it seems like guys that leave here get picked up awful fast. Maybe there's nothing to it, maybe there is." For a moment his eyes were steady on Smith's. "If there is, would you say she's part of it? Or would it be just her old man?"

Needing the lady in his business, and very soon now, Smith decided to give her a clean bill. He wouldn't have put it beyond her to cross up her own mother; certainly she was planning to cross her father, but he pretended that he believed her absolutely on the level. He cited her need for a plane. "What the hell, she doesn't have to shove these guys over the line. She collects in advance. She could bury them out in the cactus and nobody'd know the difference."

"Yeah." The burly man stood up. "Well, thanks a lot, pally."

Smith too got to his feet. "Drink?"

"Why not?"

They went over to the bar, where for a little while they stood alone except for the bartender, a man not disposed to talk nor apparently to listen while others did. The tension had not lessened in the room, but Smith sensed that he himself was no longer an object of suspicion. He and his companion were on their second round when Regan came in from the lower corridor, ostentatiously locking the door behind him. His bulldog jaw was outthrust, his skin a kind of angry magenta as he made directly for Smith. "Talk to you alone," he said. His voice had gravel in it. He looked at the bruiser. "Shove off, you."

The big man chuckled, winked broadly at Smith. "Gettin' kind of tough in his old age, ain't he?" He pushed himself from the bar, yawned widely, stretched. "Well, there's others, hey, pally?" He laughed, walked with the swaggering roll of a sailor to the nearest table, where a blackjack game was in progress. At something he said the game came to an abrupt halt.

Regan either was unaware of what was happening or didn't care. He focused slightly bloodshot eyes on Smith's face. "There's a dead man down in the wine cellar, sucker."

"Only one?" From his greater height Smith smiled down at Regan's enraged face. "That shouldn't worry a guy like you."

"And there's a bloody carpet in my girl's living-room," Regan said. He put a hand in an already bulging coat pocket. "I want to know what's going on between you two."

Smith set his empty glass down on the bar, not looking at it, looking at Regan with a smile that was now mirthless and a little cruel. "Listen, Regan, I don't owe you anything, but I'll tell you this: you're sitting on dynamite, and if you pull that gun you're going to set it off." His eyes moved briefly to where the group at the blackjack table had been joined by other groups. Some of the players were half risen from their chairs. "Don't do it, Regan."

The squat man didn't believe him. Or perhaps he was without imagination. He pulled the gun, took a backward step, leaned his left elbow on the bar. Words pushed themselves past stained, uneven teeth. "You son of a bitch!" In the absolute stillness of the room the click of the hammer under his thumb was clearly audible. Then the silence was suddenly filled with sound, animal-like, menacing. He turned and saw the pack almost on him, and losing his head, he shot the foremost man in the belly.

The lights went out.

It was like a nightmare after that, made more terrible by the utter blackness. Smith swarmed over the bar just before it collapsed under the press of men's bodies. A face came into his spread hand, a face with walrus mustaches, and he remembered that the bartender had keys. He fell on top of the man. Planks, barrels, other men fell on top of them. Hoarse shouts, curses, a swiftly stifled scream were in his ears. Regan had not shot a second time: it was easy to imagine the scream his, to visualize him being literally torn to pieces by the mob. Some of the crushing weight was suddenly gone from Smith's back and he discovered that he had the bartender's throat in his two hands. The man's fingers clawed at Smith's wrists, a knee found Smith's groin. He lifted the man's head, banged it again and again on the floor, and all the time he was conscious of the fury of sound and movement around and about him. Feet pounded up the stairs, there was the crash of breaking furniture, solid blows resounded against still more solid doors. All this in stygian, impenetrable darkness.

Quite unexpectedly the bartender went limp. Smith banged the head once more, for luck, let go of the throat beneath it and busied himself with the man's pockets. When he had the ring of keys he wriggled snakelike from under the wreckage of the bar. On hands and knees, kicked, trampled on, fallen over by other men, he moved erratically but determinedly toward the door in the far wall. Somewhere a man struck a match, and almost at Smith's ear a gun blasted. The flaming match described a parabola in the air, was blotted out for an instant, then one of the tinder-dry hangings at the windows flared brightly, illuminating a scene out of Dante.

Men with knives, fists, table legs, chairs fought their fellows without rhyme or reason. The one man they had all hated was nothing but a mass of torn clothes and flesh now, but perhaps they hadn't known this in the dark. With light they were caught in mid-motion, as when a picture stops dead on the screen. Then the burning drape dissolved in a shower of sparks and for an instant the scene was almost blotted out. But only for an instant. The sparks found lodging in a dozen places, ignited paintings, drapes, crumpled newspapers. The fire became general, the wall with the windows a continuous sheet of roaring flame, but curiously this had a co-ordinating effect on the men. Glass shattered under the impact of hurled chairs, other light pieces of furniture. Falling glass carried with it the more inflammable window coverings, and the men attacked the boards beyond. They were unmindful of the fire at their backs now; the windows promised freedom, if from nothing else, from the smoke that was suffocating them. Air sucked into the room, eddying the smoke but not dispelling it. With the air came the shrill sound of sirens.

Still on hands and knees, but very rapidly now, Smith finished his interrupted journey to the door. Half blinded with smoke and suddenly searing heat, he was making his third try with keys and lock when the door opened from without and he saw Juanita Regan standing there. A flashlight blazed in his face. She recognized him, the light went out. In her other hand she held a gun, and quite deliberately she lifted it and fired twice into the inferno behind him. "Come on, snap it up," she said. He scrambled through, stood up. She slammed the door, locked it, put her back against it. Her breathing was uneven, her eyes furious. "What happened?"

He shook his head. "Open the door."

"No."

He put a hand on her wrist. "Don't make me hurt you, baby. They've got to have that chance."

"Oh, for Christ's sake!" she said, and then, as though humoring an unreasonable child, she turned and unlocked the door and flung it open. There was no one there waiting to be let out. There was nothing but flame and smoke, and a new roaring as the door created a greater draft. But beyond all that the shouts of men and the wail of sirens were much clearer than they had been, and he knew that at least one of the windows was at last open.

"All right," he said, and together they ran down an empty silent corridor till they came to stairs, ran down them and through an echoing passage like a tunnel, where presently she unlocked an iron-bound oaken door. Beyond it was vaulted room reeking of mold and disuse and the sour-sweet smell of spilled wines. A single incandescent cast a feeble glow over a litter of broken casks and dismantled bottle racks. As they stood for a moment, panting, his eyes searched for but did not find the body that Regan had said was there, presumably that of the gross yet feminine Guadalupe. "You move him, or did poppa?"

She seemed to be listening for something outside the room they were in. "Who?"

"Lupe."

"So that's what started it!"

"Among other things," he said, and sketched in briefly the salient features of the riot and ensuing fire. "Anyway, I suppose this tears it?"

"For now," she admitted. "We may be able to pick it up later."

"You can't square your boy friend Hernandez?"

"After this?" She was scornful. "He may be dumb, but not that dumb." She looked at him. "I do hope that plane will be on time, darling."

He wiped his face on a coat sleeve. "I wish we could be as sure of getting there ourselves."

Beyond the closed door, in the passage they had just traversed, there was the scrape of shoe-leather on cement, a thud as of something heavy being put down. Taut, hand on his gun, Smith was conscious of her laughter. "It's just Manuelo with the bags, sweetheart." She opened the door.

The Mexican who came through was one Smith had not seen before. He was no longer in his prime, nor could he at any time have been called handsome, but he was powerfully built and when he looked at the girl his eyes had a kind of doglike affection in them. "The car, she is wait, chiquita." His voice was soft. "It is better that we go now, quickly." He did not look at Smith.

Smith saw that one of the bags was the pigskin case she had shown him upstairs. The other appeared equally heavy, too heavy to contain just clothing. He admired her. "You work fast, baby."

"We'll do all right," she said, and ran ahead of them to an ell from which stone steps led upward. They came out to a night full of stars only partially obscured by a drifting pall of smoke from the fire: smoke colored by leaping flames and tainted with the sickening odor of burned flesh. It seemed incredible that they were alone here; that all the noise and excitement were still confined to the front. But there were just the three of them, and across a kind of courtyard surrounded by outbuildings the car waited, without lights, but with its engine already running.

Manuelo put the bags in the rear, the girl slid under the wheel. About to climb in beside her, Smith hesitated. "Manuelo goes with us?"

"Only as far the plane, darling. We need someone to get rid of the car afterward."

"I'll ride in back," Smith decided.

She laughed at him. "Still cautious?"

"It isn't that," Smith said. "I just want to lie down and relax for a while. I'm tired."

She drove swiftly, surely, through back lanes and twisting side streets, and later across open desert, in and out among towering Joshuas, brittle sagebrush crackling against the sides of the car, under its tires. They saw no other car; no one attempted to stop them. When at last they came onto a rocky uneven road he saw that it was the one which they had first met. It seemed like a long time ago, a hell of a long time ago.

He sat up and put his watch close to his eyes. It was a few minutes before nine o'clock. He thought that over the sound of the car he could hear the muffled drum of propellers, but he was not sure. Looking backward he saw the glow of the fire still lighting up the distant sky, but here it was quite dark. Even the stars looked farther away, dim, cold.

Skirting the dunes, Juanita grew increasingly cheerful, now and then humming snatches of this or that popular tune. Beside her, Manuelo sat silent, either asleep or engrossed with private matters of his own. Smith lit a cigarette, took a deep drag, reached across the back of the seat and put it in her mouth.

"Thanks, darling." She patted his hand where it lay on her shoulder. "It won't be long now."

"No," he agreed. After a while he said: "You've got your contact lined up all right?"

"Of course"

"I ought to know a little more about what you're doing," he complained.

Briefly the cigarette in her fingers made a warning gesture toward Manuelo. "We're trying to save our necks, aren't we?" Apparently by instinct—they were still driving without lights—she found the spot she was looking for, braked the car to a halt, and cut the ignition. They sat there listening. There was a wait of no more than five minutes before they heard a plane coming in, flying low. They got out, staring upward without seeing anything. Smith reached in to the light switch, blinked the headlights once, twice. Off to the left beyond the dunes three new stars glowed the sky, winked out, shone again.

She was elated. "It's your boy friend, darling, it is, it is!" She turned and wound strong, slender arms about him. Her upturned face laughed into his. Before he could wrestle himself free of her a sledge-hammer blow from behind sent him crashing headlong into oblivion.

Chapter 17

Blazing light seared his eyeballs; new agonies attacked an already pain-raddled brain. Retching, he leaned far forward and tried to throw up, but he could not. In his mouth was a sour, nauseous taste that said he had been sick before, perhaps more than once. He dicovered that he was handcuffed. Reflected light from the steel bracelets on his wrists stabbed at his eyes. Beyond his imprisoned hands were men's feet in shoes uniformly alike; the trousers above them were uniform trousers. He was in jail.

A hand came into his range of vision, fingers spread. It smothered his face, flung him roughly erect in the chair. The room tilted, began to whirl. He was surrounded by a maelstrom of voices, lights, a great rushing sound like wind in trees or a giant waterfall, then gratefully darkness descended again.

This time when he awakened, it was to the sharp bite of ammonia in his nostrils, his throat. He gagged, tried to avoid the insistent demand on his consciousness. He did not open his eyes.

"Breathe deeply," someone commanded. "Through the mouth."

And when he refused to co-operate another voice said: "He is stubborn, that one." There was general laughter. He was suddenly drenched from head to foot with icy water. He came out of that gasping, shivering as with the ague. He could no longer pretend to be asleep. Surprisingly, though, after the first shock was over, he felt a little better. He mopped at his streaming face clumsily, because of his fettered wrists. He saw that he was in a room he recognized: the office of Captain Rodriguez Dolores Hernandez. The handsome captain himself was there, leaning against the desk, behind which sat an older, less handsome man. This one had short-cropped grizzled hair, fierce grizzled mustaches, and a seamed, pockmarked face. He bore a considerable resemblance to Joseph Stalin. Three other men, one of them still holding the bucket that had doused Smith, made up the room's complement of cops. Beyond the closed door other men seemed to be doing a great deal of running around: there was the clatter of feet, of telegraph instruments, the clack of voices. Full memory returned to Smith with a rush. Lips that were numb, seemingly swollen to twice normal thickness, formed the word: "Phone." He lurched awkwardly from the chair. "Gotta telephone."

Two of the men seized him by the arms, forced him back down again. Stalin's double looked at Hernandez as though for an interpretation of what Smith had said. He appeared puzzled. Hernandez, smiling, gave him a free translation. "He no doubt wishes an attorney." They both found considerable amusement in this. The three underlings felt that they should join in the merriment. They laughed uproariously.

Smith saw by the clock on the wall that it was almost eleven. He had been out for well over an hour. Vaguely, as from a half-remembered dream, he knew that he had not been completely blotto all that time. He seemed to recall other awakenings, one of them in a street noisy with confusion and many men; staggering blindly, drunkenly along this street, he was suddenly engaged in a brief furious battle, which abruptly ended in nothingness.

He licked his lips, forced them to enunciate clearly, though Hernandez's face swam before his eyes like a reflection in rippled water. "Important—contact Federal Narcotics Division—San Diego." After a moment he said: "Please."

"And why do you wish this, señor?"

"Because I—" Again he moistened parched, puffy lips. His eyes sought an unbiased intelligence among the five men before him. Not finding one, he went ahead anyway. Time was of the essence now. "It is necessary that she be stopped. Failing that, I have information that may help them find her."

Hernandez's handsome face swam into sharp focus. "Who, señor?"

"Juanita Regan."

A back-handed blow rocked his head far over, but curiously sharpened his vision. Hernandez's voice was smooth, mocking. "So all is to be blamed on the missing Señorita Regan. What have you done with her, señor?"

"What have I done with her?" He had the crazy impulse to laugh, but the sound that issued from his lips was not laughter. "Listen, I'm trying to tell you that she has stolen a plane belonging to the United States government. She may or may not have murdered the pilot. She murdered at least one other man that I know of, a gambler from Tia Juana called El Guadalupe."

Hernandez laughed, addressed the bulky, morose man behind the desk. "You see, *coronel?*" Triumphantly he returned his attention to Smith. "It was you, not she, who killed Señor Guadalupe."

"What makes you think that?" Smith lifted his hands and in spite of the steel bracelets managed to massage some of the pain from his throbbing temples. "Or don't you think it? You're just making it up as you go along?" He fended aside a second swipe from Hernandez's fist, spoke rapidly to Hernandez's superior. "Look, this guy is in love with the girl. She's played him for a sap and he's still too much of a sap to admit it. Make him lay off me."

The colonel got up and came around the desk. He put his face down close to Smith's. His voice was guttural, impassioned. He wanted it distinctly understood, he said, that he *el jefe de policía,* was not in love with anybody except his wife, and anyway this was beside the point. So was all this business of airplanes, Narcotics Divisions, and so on. The simple fact was that Smith was a known and much-wanted criminal named Eduardo McSweeney, and that he was not dealing with foolish gringos. He was dealing with Mexico, specifically with that portion of it known as Los Gatos, Baja California, where the police were not so stupid as the gringo supposed. He began pacing, his feet falling solidly to accent his words. Did Señor McSweeney think that they in Los Gatos were not fully as scientific as any police in the world? Did he think that there were no ballistics experts in Mexico? He paused in his bombast, addressed Smith more quietly, as one reasoning man to another. "Come, señor, we have taken from you a pistol. It is the same pistol which ends the life of our fellow national El Guadalupe. Let us have no more lies."

Smith could recognize a spot when he saw it, and this was it. By the simple expedient of switching pistols Juanita had framed him for the murder of another of her dupes and left him to be shot or picked up by a third, Captain Rodriguez Dolores Hernandez. He decided that her thoroughness, her adaptability, amounted to genius. Faced with the sudden and unexpected collapse of a long-term project, she had picked up the most important pieces—including him, until she was sure he had produced the promised plane—and then scuttled him with an admirable singleness of purpose. He did not know how she had got over the hurdle of Jerry, the plane's pilot, but he would have given you tremendous odds that she had; that right now, as of this moment, she was sitting safe and snug somewhere in the States, happily counting the loot she would now not have to divide with anybody. Her one error, though he could not even be sure of this, was that she had believed him an outlaw named McSweeney. He addressed himself earnestly to *el jefe.* "If it is as you say, then surely there can be no harm in a message to San Diego. You will still have me, no?"

Hernandez pounded the desk in an access of rage. "Madre de Dios, it is but another trick, I tell you! Do not listen to him, *mi coronel.*"

Smith did not take his eyes from the chief's pockmarked face. "It is true that I tricked the captain in the matter of my identity. My brother officer who was here today also played a trick, but it was because of things we knew which said Hernandez was either a crook or a fool." He jingled the fetters on his wrists. "Look, colonel, there's going to be a lot of publicity over the fire and the thieves and murderers who found shelter in Los Gatos. I believe that you are an honest man, that even Hernandez may have been used without his knowledge. But will others believe it?" He shook his head. "Your choice is between being called a bribe-taker, an ass, or a very smart man."

He saw that he had made a slight impression. Hernandez saw it too. "I implore you, do not listen to him. He tries to create international complications, perhaps to be extradited so that we may not punish him for that which occurs in our own domain."

Smith looked at him. "She said you were dumb." He laughed. "But even she didn't think you were dumb enough to go believing in her after the blow-off. That's why she ran away. She ran away carrying a hundred thousand dollars' worth of narcotics, for which she murdered one man, possibly more than one."

Hernandez's skin became an ugly, unhealthy yellow. "Liar," he said. "Liar." But his voice lacked conviction, and presently he went around the desk and sat down and put his chin in his hands. His eyes avoided the eyes of the others in the room.

El jefe studied Smith intently. "Of what import, this message you wish delivered?"

Smith looked at the avidly interested faces of the three constables. "This is a matter of discretion. Perhaps—"

Hernandez lifted his head. "Do not send the men away, *coronel.*"

"All right," Smith said, "the hell with discretion." He drew a slow breath. "Anyone in the Narcotics Bureau will do. Tell them this: if Miss Regan is not already in custody, she may try to contact either a George Falconer or a Christopher Lancaster. Remember those names. They are important." He looked sidewise at Hernandez. "*El capitán* can probably describe Miss Regan more intimately than I."

"And you, señor?" The colonel's voice was suddenly smooth, suave. "I shall, perhaps, mention that you are under arrest?"

"If you do," Smith said, "and what I think has happened has happened, they'll be damned glad of it. They'll probably give you a medal for shooting me."

Chapter 18

The cell stank. It stank mostly of long and continuous occupancy by unwashed human bodies, but there were other smells too. A leaky faucet in the concrete wall at the rear of the cell dripped incessantly into an open trap, which must also have been intended for the latrine. At least it had been used for that, and there was no sign of any other. The blanket and lumpy straw tick on the steel bunk hinted of crawling things, but he sat on it anyway and waited for the giddiness in his head to subside. The feet of the guards who had brought him scraped along the concrete corridor between rows of cells, and for a little while there was no other sound. Then a door clanged shut and the cell block came alive with the curses and laughter of men, and ribald shouted greetings to the newcomer in their midst. He had been through it all before. Not here, but in other jails as bad or worse.

His fingers tenderly explored the tumor-like swelling at the base of his skull. It was soft, yielding to the touch, and beneath it where bone should be he could not feel anything solid. He quit poking at it, for fear his brains would leak out. And then he thought: "What brains?" A kind of crazy croaking laughter issued from his mouth. His mouth felt funny too, as though someone had pounded it with a wooden mallet. Maybe they had.

Presently, over the sound of voices and shuffling feet, the drip of water impinged on his consciousness and he realized that he was thirsty. He got up and went unsteadily to the faucet. Clinging to it, he bent far over and put his mouth to the outlet and twisted the valve. Water gushed into his mouth, out over his face and neck. He turned his face downward, flooded head and shoulders. After a while he went back to his bunk and took off his coat and shirt and used the drier portion of the shirt to wipe his face and neck and hands. He felt better.

A guard with a riot gun came along the passage and looked in at him. "You would like something to eat, señor? Cigarettes? A newspaper, perhaps?"

Smith discovered that he still had money. He put a five-dollar bill into an outstretched brown hand. "Cigarettes," he said. "And some aspirin if you can find it." The guard went away

In the cell directly opposite, a man got off the bunk and

came to stand at the bars, peering across at Smith through eyes that were almost swollen shut. He was the bruiser with the cauliflower ear and badly set broken nose, though these were only minor disfigurements now. His face was a mass of welts and lacerations. The hands that gripped the bars on either side of the face were raw with broken blister. His eyebrows were gone, as was the hair along one whole side of his scalp. "Hello, pally." His voice sounded as though someone had him by the throat, but neither the fire nor his captors had beaten all the humor out of him. "Well, this is different anyhow, hey?"

"I'm glad you like it," Smith said.

"I didn't say I liked it." With a thumb and finger he managed to open one eye a little wider. "But I'm the kind that can take it as it comes, and anyway we got that bastard Regan."

"The Old Philosopher program," Smith said.

The guard came back with cigarettes, matches, a ten-cent tin of aspirin. He did not offer any change from the five-dollar bill, but that was all right, Smith hadn't expected any. He was grateful to whoever had carelessly left him the money in the first place. He took four of the tablets, drank some more water, lit a cigarette. He divided the remaining loot equally, made a little bundle of half knotted into a handkerchief, and tossed it to the man in the opposite cell.

"Thanks, pally."

For a little while they smoked in silence, companionably, though two sets of bars and eight feet of concrete passage lay between them. Then Smith said: "Any of the others get away?"

"Three or four ain't showed yet. They got most of us." Puffy broken lips luxuriously expelled a cloud of smoke. "From what I hear, a couple won't ever show. I tried to go back in after 'em, but the goddam cholo coppers knocked me over, so I couldn't."

Smith thought that you met heroism in the damnedest places. He wondered if the pockmarked chief of police had finally decided to telephone. He was still wondering about this when after a second cigarette he presently fell asleep.

Two or three times during the night he awakened to a drowsy realization of where he was; to the snores and mutterings of other men in adjacent cells. Once he was very cold and he thought about putting on his coat, but before he got around to it he was asleep again. He did not know it was daylight when the guard and another policeman roused him and led him stumbling along the passage and through a steel-barred door, which clanged shut behind them. They went through another door, this time of wood, and then bright sunlight struck his eyes, blinding him, and he stood there swaying a little between the two men, but not really feeling too bad. It was just the suddenness of the awakening and all that light after what seemed, by comparison, to have been total darkness.

"Well," a dry, emotionless voice said, "you're quite a mess, aren't you?" He did not need to open his eyes to identify the owner of the voice. It was the big shot himself, variously known as Mister Gregg, the Gray Man, the Old Man, and "that son of a bitch."

Smith admitted that he must indeed be a mess. He said he felt like a mess. He saw that there were others in the room besides himself and the gray man and the two guards. Over by one of the barred windows *el coronel* stood, arms folded, his pockmarked face heavy with lack of sleep. Captain Hernandez was talking to a round-bellied little man with pink, childlike skin and combed-cotton hair who turned out to be a United States vice-consul. Brick Cassidy was straddling the seat of a chair, his arms crossed on its back, his eyes interestedly examining the assortment of contusions and abrasions on Smith's face. He said: "Boy, when they mace you down here they mace you but good, don't they?"

"What did you expect after the build-up I had?" Smith stared without affection at the gray man. "Well, did you get her or didn't you?"

Gregg seemed to have some little difficulty with his breathing. "No," he said presently. "No, we didn't get her. There seems to be a slight discrepancy here somewhere. She was to have taken the plane?"

Smith glared at him "She did take it!"

The gray man shook his head, no. "Sorry, you'll have to revise that part of it." His voice was politely regretful. "Jerry came back empty, quite alone."

Smith was incredulous. "He couldn't have, damn it! There'd have been no sense to what happened if—"

"Maybe he couldn't have," the gray man said tiredly. "He did." He drew a deep breath. "You see how awkward that makes it. If part of your story doesn't hold water, none of it does. We might have covered up for you if we'd known the exact circumstances, but unfortunately the message we got was based on a premise we already knew to be false."

Quite suddenly Smith began to shake. He was not frightened; he was angry, angrier than he had been in years. "Then you did nothing about it? You just laughed Lancaster and Falconer off on the theory that I was crazy?"

"Not quite. They're under surveillance, but only because we can't afford to miss even the semblance of a chance." He sighed gently. "Now about this Guadalupe murder—tell me exactly what happened."

"Well, it was like this," Smith said. "I don't like queers. Never did. They do things to me. So when I ran into this one and he made his proposition I saw red and up and shot him." He laughed at the look on Cassidy's face. "You know how it is when you see red." His own face was suddenly congested, his voice choked with rage. "Listen, you bastards, I won't tell you a God-damned thing till I talk to Jerry!"

The gray man gave Cassidy a nod. "Get him."

Cassidy got up and went out. The colonel, Hernandez, and the smallish, round-bellied man came over. The two guards retired to stand before the door through which they had led Smith. The colonel addressed Gregg. "Well, señor?"

"He is our man, colonel. Beyond that I know nothing."

"You do not accept responsibility for his acts?"

"How can I? I don't know what the acts, alleged or otherwise, have been."

"That's all right," Smith said. "I'll confess to anything."

The colonel ignored him. Eyes like obsidian remained intent on the gray man's face. "But he came to Los Gatos with your knowledge—at your instigation?"

The vice-consul was suddenly a very worried man. "I don't like this. I don't like it a little bit." His voice had the sound of Iowa corn country in it. "The State Department cannot take cognizance—will not go on record as interfering—"

The gray man looked at him. "We never have had any help from you people. We've learned not to expect it." He returned his attention to the chief of police. "I do not ordinarily employ threats, Colonel Machado, nor do I like them tossed at me. But there's a planeload of reporters and news photographers waiting outside. Which story do you think they'll find most interesting, our operations inside your back yard, or the one about how much your back yard needed cleaning?" He trimmed and lit one of his thin, dappled cigars. "Another thing: I don't say you can't make this murder charge stick. Considering that the body showed evidence of torture, it's obviously murder. Against an outlaw named McSweeney you'd have little difficulty. Against a

Federal officer you're going to have to dig up a satisfactory motive for such a killing. Do you think you can do it?"

The colonel was not a man to be intimidated. "Look you, señor, by your man's own account there is much money involved here. Perhaps if we had the Señorita Regan, or could by other means corroborate Señor Smith's story, it would be as you say. But in the absence of these, the money itself supplies sufficient motive." His smile had a lot of teeth in it, but it was not exactly pleasant. "It will not be the first time an officer of the law has—what you call—sold out."

Captain Hernandez appeared to find something highly amusing in this, possibly because he himself had been suspected of selling out. Smith found nothing at all amusing in it; without the slightest strain his imagination conjured up a picture of a firing squad with him as the target. The gray man too seemed to find the immediate prospect depressing. For a moment he looked even grayer than usual. Then he opened his mouth to say something, closed it abruptly as Cassidy came in with Jerry Bittner.

Jerry had his head half turned, was laughing at some remark of Cassidy's. A somewhat dilapidated Air Force cap sat rakishly over one ear. He might have been a kid in his late teens. He saw Smith. Shock, incredulity, the swift shadow of fear chased the laughter from his blue eyes. He stopped so suddenly that Cassidy bumped him from behind. "They didn't tell me— Well, hello!" The heartiness in his voice had a forced sound to it.

Smith was assailed by a curious emptiness in the pit of his stomach, a trembling of the knees. "You didn't expect to see me, Jerry? Why?"

The boy spoke through stiff lips. "I—I don't know. I guess because you didn't—show last night."

"It wasn't because she told you I was dead? That would have been very like her," Smith said. He wished to God somebody else had this chore. He forced himself to go on with it. "Listen, kid, I know that baby. I know just about what she would have said to you." He laughed harshly. "For a little while I worried myself sick, thinking she might have knocked you off, but that wasn't necessary, was it? She's a great little talker." He took a quick forward step, put his face down close to the boy's. "Where is she, kid?"

"I don't—" Jerry backed away, looked at the others in the room with eyes that were suddenly blank, like a sleepwalker's. "I don't get this. What are you trying to do to me?"

Smith thrust him roughly into a chair. "God damn it, where is she?"

The gray man interfered. "Wait a minute, maybe we're going at this the wrong way."

"The wrong way?" Smith sneered at him. "Either he knows where she is or she suckered him like she did me and half a hundred others. There's no doubt at all that she went with him in the first place." He stood over the boy, with only a corner of the scarred oak table intervening. "Look, kid, I was there when you came down. It was my signal you answered. And I can tell you almost word for word what she said when you picked her up. She said: 'McSweeney's dead, darling. Now there'll be just the two of us. Just you and Juanita and all that lovely money.' "

A hoarse cry as of physical agony broke from the boy's lips. He put his face in his hands and began to sob. They watched him with curiously strained, almost embarrassed faces. It was as though they did not want to look at him, but preferred that to looking at each other. After a while, after the first horrible paroxysm was over, he began to speak in disjointed, broken phrases. He did not lift his head, but stared dully at a point on the floor just beyond his feet. "She told me you had been caught in the fire," he said. "I understand that you had thrown in with her—she made it sound so damned plausible—"

"She knew I was a Fed?"

"I don't think so—not now. I guess she kind of tricked me into admitting— Anyway, it didn't seem to matter when she found out what I was." He shivered, wiped his mouth on the back of a hand. "All right, so I went for it, and for her. I don't know whether I'd have done it for just the dough—maybe I would have—my cut would've been more than I could earn in ten years. But with her thrown in—well, you know what she was like."

"Yes," Smith said, "I know what she was like." Then he said: "Was?" He seized the boy's shoulders, jerked him erect. His voice was savage. "What the hell happened? What did you do with her?"

Jerry's blue eyes regarded him without surprise, without anger. There seemed to be nothing at all back of the dull, somnambulistic stare. "She suckered me," he said. "The idea was that if I didn't report in I'd have the law on my tail the rest of my life." Something that might have been a laugh issued from between bloodless lips. "So I sat her down beside a highway into town—her and her expensive luggage—and took off for the port."

"Good God!" Cassidy said. "Just like that?"

"You don't know her," the boy said. "I hope you meet her sometime." He looked without rancor at the ring of faces around him. "Naturally, the address she gave me was a phony."

Chapter 19

It turned out that there was nothing wrong with Smith that a doctor, a Turkish bath, and a barber couldn't fix. He was in his own room, recovering from the last of these and laying out fresh clothes, when Cassidy came in carrying a bottle and the early editions of the evening papers.

"Hi, murderer," Cassidy said cheerfully. He proffered the bottle. "A token of good will from our esteemed chief."

"I don't want any part of it," Smith said. "Or any more of his master-minding, either. I'm sick of this rat race." As a result of alternate hot towels soaked in epsom salts and cold towels saturated in astringent witch hazel his face was pale, composed, numb.

Cassidy admired the barber's handiwork. "A little rouge on those waxen cheeks and you'd go over big in a coffin." He held out the bottle enticingly. "You sure you wouldn't care for a sup of this lovely formaldehyde?"

"No."

"Poppa will be hurt."

"Hah."

"Well, he will," Cassidy insisted. He went into the bathroom, returning presently with two tumblers half full of golden liquor. "Here. He didn't send it. I just made that up."

Smith accepted the glass ungraciously. "Don't think you're kidding anybody." He took a tentative sip. "The method may be yours. The idea of your coming here was his."

Cassidy admitted this without embarrassment. "The trouble with you, you're just a goddam perfectionist. You're worse than the Old Man. The least little thing goes wrong, you get sore."

"The least little thing," Smith said. He held his glass to the light, watching the bead form on its contents. "Like Jerry, you mean?"

"Yeah, that son of a bitch."

Smith looked at him quickly. "I wasn't thinking of him in

quite that way. I was thinking of how we deliberately make wild men out of kids, give 'em the Air Medal or maybe the Congressional for being wild, then expect them to level off afterward as though nothing had happened." He emptied his glass, shuddered. "What makes you think you wouldn't have done the same thing? Or me? Does carrying a badge immunize us or something?"

"I'll bite," Cassidy said. "Why didn't you? You had the same opportunity."

"How do you know I didn't?"

"Jesus, you'd better have another drink, bud."

"I'll tell you why I didn't," Smith said. "The only reason. It's just that I don't give a damn for money. I'm fine the way I am. Moral scruples, allegiance to the flag, all that pap—how do you know what they mean till you've got something to balance against them?"

Cassidy banged the bottle down on the dresser. His face was beet-red. "What the hell's got into you?"

"I'm sore," Smith said. "You know how it is. You said it yourself. The least little thing makes me fly into a tizzy." He poured himself a good stiff slug of the Scotch, carried it over to one of the twin beds, and lay flat on his belly. " 'Go down there,' the man says, 'on account of you speak Spanish.' Listen, I didn't speak six words of Spanish the whole God-damned time I was in that flea trap!"

"You're a heller with matches, though," Cassidy opened one of the papers, displayed the banner headline: "FIRE GUTS MILLION DOLLAR HOTEL!"

"That was two other guys," Smith said. He attempted to drink from his glass while lying on his stomach. It was impossible. He propped himself on an elbow. His face was no longer sullen. "Read me some more sentences with guts in them."

Cassidy cleared his throat noisily. " 'Federal Narcotics agents today disclosed for the first time the existence of an international dope ring whose tentacles'—"

"Whose what?"

"Don't get dirty," Cassidy said. He perused the paper in silence for a moment. "It says here: 'Working in conjunction with Mexican authorities.' Boy, did you work in conjunction with those greasers!" He laid the sheet aside, said casually: "The Old Man certainly did a good job of tidying up after you."

"Oh God, yes. They still think I knocked off Lupe."

"You're free, aren't you?"

"Temporarily," Smith conceded. "As a matter of fact, their case against me is better than the one against the lady. Even if she's picked up, it's my word against hers, and after all I didn't actually see her shoot him."

"You'll make a fine witness for the defense," Cassidy said. "What about Jerry's testimony?"

"A good lawyer could get that thrown out too." Smith rolled over on his back, juggled his replenished glass on his chest. "No, my hearty, so long as she isn't caught with the stuff in her possession, or in the middle of some brand-new job, she'll probably go scot-free. With those legs and those eyes she could make a jury believe anything, even that her association with her father was due to coercion, her utter, abject fear of him."

Cassidy's eyes glistened. "I'd like to meet that babe. Not just for business reasons, either." He asked the same question the burly man with the broken nose had asked.

"I don't know," Smith said. "What with this and that I somehow never got around to finding out."

"That's your story," Cassidy leered. He brought the bottle over to the bedside. "Another small one?"

"That's right," Smith said, "ply me with liquor till I'm all soft inside, till I'm just like putty in your—his—hands." From beneath lowered lids his eyes watched Cassidy's face. "What'd he send you to find out—how much I neglected to tell him?"

Cassidy was offended. "Certainly not."

"That's good," Smith said. This time he did not have to raise his head to pour liquor into his mouth. "I thought maybe he was afraid I'd break this case without benefit of his guiding genius."

"Reed, for God's sake, the Old Man hasn't got a crystal ball. He can't foresee everything that happens!"

"Go on, defend him," Smith said petulantly. "It isn't you he thought was a murderer. It isn't you who struggled in Delilah's arms while that son of a bitch Manuelo struck him—me—from behind." He saw that his glass was once more empty. "Thieves?" he said. "Thieves? Around here?"

"Come on, you're not that drunk. What are you going to do?"

Smith appeared to think this over. "Sleep?"

"Damn it, you know what I mean. About the case."

"Oh, that." He wriggled his shoulders into a more comfortable position. "In good time I shall probably solve it.

Single-handed and without assistance from the master mind and his hired help."

Something like triumph glittered in Cassidy's eyes. "Now we're getting somewhere." He put his face down close to Smith's. "What have you got that we don't know about?"

"Not halitosis anyway," Smith said, and pushed Cassidy away. "Why don't you answer the telephone?"

Cassidy did this, presently smothered the instrument against his chest, and looked across at the long, thin man on the bed. "It's your girl friend."

"Which one? I'm just lousy with them."

"Lotsa Dough. Miss Gotrocks."

"I'm not in."

"He says he's not in," Cassidy reported to the phone. "How's about some wiener schnitzel and a short beer with me instead?" He hung up dispiritedly. "I don't know what that girl sees in you."

"Character," Smith said. The glass rolled off his chest and he caught it deftly. He opened his eyes very wide. "Listen, sweet pimp, go back and tell the unfeeling monster who sent you that I wouldn't tell him if I did, but I don't. Tell him that all I have is a small amount of pride and a yen to get my hands on a certain young lady's throat. Tell him that if he has any ideas such as sending me to British Columbia because I happen to speak English I prefer to be shot by Colonel Machado's barefoot constabulary." His smile was amiably satanic. "Any more questions?"

"One," Cassidy said. "Was your mother married?"

Someone knocked, and when Smith showed no disposition to move from the bed, Cassidy went to the door, opened it. Linda stood there. "I'm working my way through college. Would you care to buy any brushes, magazines, my virginity, or a vacuum cleaner?" She peered past Cassidy into the dimness of the room. It was now almost dark outside. "Pardon me, is that a man in there or should I call the house detective?"

"You might as well let her in," Smith said. "The rich are insensitive to insults."

Cassidy snapped on the lights, stood aside. "I hope you can make better progress with him than I have."

"Oh, a competitor." She came in, bringing with her the scent of violets and the fresh outdoors. "Are you working your way through college too?"

Smith stood up, drawing his robe tighter about him. "He's been trying to sell me on a life of shame. He's a procurer."

Cassidy reddened. "Listen, I— Ah, the hell with it!" He gave Linda a brisk nod, went out, banging the door behind him. She looked after him, looked inquiringly at Smith. "Now what was that all about?"

"I irritate people," Smith said. "It's a knack." He helped her off with her furs. "Do make yourself at home, now that you insist on being here." He found the bottle, a clean glass. "Drink?"

"Your hospitality overwhelms me," she said. She accepted the glass, moved it over to the windows, and stood looking down into the street, now noisy with traffic. She had a very pale beige dress with flaring skirt, a broad-belted high waistline, and militarily squared shoulders. Her gloves, shoes, hat, all looked, as usual, tailored expressly to go with the dress. Still with her back to him she said: "I read about the Los Gatos exposé. Do you mind very much if I had to find out whether you were alive or dead?"

"No."

"Just plain old 'No'?"

He did not say anything. After a time she turned and looked at him. "How was she?"

He pretended he didn't know what she was talking about. "Who?"

"The mystery woman." As though she had memorized it she recited an accurate description of Juanita Regan. "I had to get that from the papers too."

"Sorry," he said stiffly. "I should have made my report in triplicate." He lit a cigarette, exhaled twin gusts of smoke. "People keep asking me about her. I hardly know what to say any more."

She tossed off her drink, quickly, as a man would. Her face was pale. "All right, you don't owe me anything."

"That's where you're wrong, precious. Your coming down there without being invited damned near got me killed." He drew a slow breath. "We clown around a lot among ourselves, but you have to learn when not to do it."

"I see."

"No, you don't," he said angrily. "Granted the information you had was of some value to me, the way you got it, what might have happened if things had turned out differently— Listen, damn it, these people don't play like ladies and gentlemen. I've got all I can do to think about myself and them, without having to worry about you too." He began pacing the room, his terry-cloth robe swishing about his calves on the turns. "You think you've got a feud with the people who used you, who sucked you into this mess. Maybe you feel you owe us something for Harry Gee. Maybe you think that by playing amateur detective—and God knows you couldn't do worse than we alleged professionals—you can trap me into a serious entanglement with you." He laughed harshly. His mien was harsh, cruel. "A true wifely interest in her man's work, that sort of thing." He came and stood before her. "Give it up, Linda. I'm no good for you. Leave it lay."

She bowed her head a little. "You're right, of course." When she looked at him her eyes were clear, golden, faintly amused. "We spoiled darlings have got to be taught we can't have everything." She went around him, picked up her furs. "Well, it's been an experience, Mr. Smith."

Abruptly he felt an emptiness inside him, an emptiness that over the years no other stress had occasioned. A trembling seized him and in an effort to keep it out of his voice, perhaps kidding himself that it wasn't there at all, he spoke carefully, quietly. "Listen to me. There are four men dead, four that I know about, since this thing started. A guy we trusted went wrong. One of the dead men had his fingernails pulled out as he lay dying. I don't say that will happen to you. I say it could happen. Especially it could happen if circumstances made it necessary to put pressure on me, and it was known the way I feel about you." He realized his error the moment the words were out. The sudden quiver of her mouth, the bright unshed tears in her eyes, were too much for him. "Oh Christ," he said in a discouraged voice, and took her in his arms.

Chapter 20

As he was putting Linda into her car at a little after eight o'clock that evening a Police Department sedan pulled up in the loading zone under the hotel marquee. Captain Dietrich got out and came over. "Well," he said, "congratulations!"

Smith looked at him blankly. "On what?"

"On a number of things." Dietrich wore joviality like an unaccustomed cloak. "Mainly being alive, I guess. I understand you had kind of a tough time down there."

"So-so," Smith said.

Dietrich took off his hat, nodded affably in Linda. "Evening, Miss Van Owen. Your father is well?"

"Quite well," she assured him.

He laughed. "There's no need to ask how you are." He jerked his head at Smith. "Or him, either. I thought he might be mourning the loss of his lovely redhead, but at his age and with your own radiant self to comfort him—"

"Don't overdo it," Smith said. "You haven't the brouge for it."

Dietrich brushed his short, bristly mustache with a blunt index finger. "Well, I was just passing by. Anything new at your end?"

Smith shook his head. "Haven't you heard? The master mind and I had a disagreement. I'm sulking."

"Oh? What about?"

"This and that. You, for one thing." He held up a hand as the older man bridled. "Not you personally, but this business of a general alarm." He told Dietrich much the same thing he had told Cassidy. "By this time she's done what she had to do, or been scared off doing it. Certainly the receiving end will know she's hot. They wouldn't take delivery for free. My guess is if the deal hasn't already been closed, she'll bury the stuff and walk into headquarters just to laugh in your faces. A smart shyster could spring her in half an hour."

"You sound like a pretty fair mouthpiece yourself," Dietrich said. The iron was back in his voice, though he tried to mask it with a chuckle. "You haven't been advising her, have you?"

"Sure." Smith held up two crossed fingers. "We're just like that. I'm the guy you're really looking for, but I'm smart, see? I've got the stuff in my pocket right now."

With a visible effort Dietrich held on to his temper. "Then you're not working?"

"What the hell is there for me to do?" Smith demanded. "There's a thousand of you cops already running around peering under beds."

"All right," Dietrich said, "how about Falconer and"—his eyes slid sidewise to Linda's profile—"this other guy?"

"Well, what about them? Why don't you go knock them over and ask *them* where she is? Or where the stuff is? You're wasting your time on me."

Dietrich appealed to Linda. "I'm damned if I know why it is, ma'am, but no matter how we start off, him and me, we always end up at each other's throats. Can you explain that to me?"

"I think he just hates cops," Linda said. "Himself included." And to Smith: "Why don't you be nice to the man?"

Smith's face grew dark with repressed fury. "Because he's following the same line as Gregg and Cassidy and all the rest of them. Either I'm holding out vital information—for God knows what purpose, unless I'm just plain crooked—or I'm getting ready to welsh on my testimony." He glared at Dietrich. "Isn't that about it?"

Dietrich made a fist of his right hand, looked at it thoughtfully. "Someday," he said, "I'm going to have the pleasure of nailing you to the cross. I can hardly wait." He turned and strode hard-heeled to his car, got in, and slammed the door. With the siren wide open he backed into a traffic lane, reversed, and went roaring down the street.

Linda made disparaging noises. "Such tempers," she said. "The both of you. You ought to be ashamed."

Smith gave her a sheepish grin. "I know, but they keep on needling me." He began to laugh. "Did you ever see anything funnier than Dietrich trying to carry the Blarney Stone on his back?" In an affected, comedy-Irish dialect he said, "Your own radiant self, is it?"

She was not amused. "I had reason to be radiant, until a little while ago. I thought—" she moved as though to slide over under the wheel. "Well, thanks for the dinner and—so on."

"Now who's being nasty?" He leaned in the open window, found her mouth with his. "We'll work it out, sweetheart. I may even decide to become a vice-president in one of your father's companies."

"Good night, Reed."

"Good night, precious."

When she had gone, he stood for a moment watching the dwindling taillights of the Cadillac till they could no longer be distinguished from other taillights in the maelstrom of traffic. Then, buttoning his topcoat, he went back through the lobby and down to the hotel garage, where he got his own car.

The exit gave onto a side street bisecting the busier boulevard, but even here traffic was reasonably heavy and he had to straddle the sidewalk while three or four cars crossed his path trying to beat the signal at the corner. He in turn frustrated a couple of pedestrians, who finally went around behind him, and then noticed a third who showed no evidence of going anywhere at all, just stood there looking at him. He recognized the man as the larger of George Falconer's two bodyguards. At the same instant a sleek black limousine drew up even with the driveway, effectively blocking it. Short-but-durable got out of the driver's seat and moved leisurely to Smith's other side. Around a toothpick in the corner of his mouth he spoke to his weightier companion. "Whatsa matter, he giving you an argument?"

"Nah, I ain't even ast him yet."

"Well, ask him."

Neither of them seemed at all concerned about passersby or other cars beginning to pile up behind their own. Neither seemed at all worried about Smith himself. He might have been an inanimate object they were discussing. Something that Linda had said recurred to him: that if he were upset and on edge because of unforeseen developments, the opposition certainly had reason to be that way too. Until now he hadn't believed it.

Hefty opened the left-hand door. "Come on, pally. George wants talk to you." He jerked his head toward the stalled limousine.

"No," Smith said.

"No?"

"No," Smith said firmly. "Shoot if you must this old gray head, if George wants to talk to me he can jolly well get out and come over here. I visited in his car last."

Hefty looked speculatively at two men and a woman who had passed, apparently thinking they had but a moment to wait. "You folks tryna get a earful or somep'n?"

They detoured hastily. They went clear out into the street to do it. Horns were beginning to honk now, impatiently, and there was considerable backing and filling among cars trying to get out of the jammed lane into a free one. A uniformed policeman came lumbering down from the corner. "What's this? What's all this, now?"

Short-and-durable jockeyed the toothpick to the other side of his mouth. "Hi, copper." Gold teeth made his smile brilliant. "Why don't you make those monkeys quit their yakking? It gets on George's nerves." He turned his back, swaggering over to the limousine. For an appreciable moment the policeman just stood there, slack-jawed with astonishment. Then, furiously, he bellowed: "Hey, you!" and ran after the short thick man.

Falconer got out of the limousine's tonneau, bulky, unhurried. The policeman's attitude lost its truculence, became respectful. Hefty, still with one hand on the car door next to Smith, said admiringly: "That cop's gonna go far. Yes sir, he might even be a sergeant someday."

Smith conceded that this was likely. He was sure of it when the patrolman took up his stance in the middle of the street and with whistle and epithet began sorting out the traffic snarl. The sleek black limousine stayed right where it was. Short-but-durable leaned on a fender picking his teeth and interestedly watching the proceedings. Falconer, his broad face smooth, pink, impassive, crossed the sidewalk. "You're a stubborn man, Smith." He nodded dismissal to Hefty, who retired a distance of perhaps six feet. "This is the second time I've called on you. I hope the third won't be necessary."

"If it is," Smith said, "I'll bet it won't be so public. Still, if all our cops are like that one, I guess it wouldn't make much difference." He muffled a minor belch with a polite hand. "Ulcers," he explained. "The doctors keep saying they're not, but I know better. It can't all be radishes." He pretended to look for sympathy in Falconer's face. Finding none, he said: "As a matter of fact, you could have saved yourself the trouble this time. I was just on my way to see you."

"Indeed?" Gloved fingers carried Falconer's cigar to his mouth; the aroma of dollar Havana was rich, full-bodied. "There are already about six of you guys on my doorstep." He shook his head, deploring this condition. "Bad for my business. Bad for anybody's business, but especially mine." He drew on the cigar carefully, thoughtfully. "A gambler's customers are a scary lot. They take fright easy. Between the local johns and you boys— Well, I'd like to put an end to it, and that's a fact."

"I'll write Washington tonight," Smith said.

Falconer's cold eyes regarded him steadily, intently. "I'm not kidding, Smith."

"Neither am I," Smith said. "How did you know I was a Fed?"

Falconer's expression did not change. "Word gets around, soldier. What am I supposed to be, deaf, dumb, and blind?"

"You knew it the other night."

"Maybe. I won't say yes and I won't say no."

"That's the trouble with you smart bastards," Smith complained. "You're only half smart. You keep clinging to that moth-eaten old adage about honor and thieves." He found and lit a cigarette, blew out the match. "This Regan lovely, for instance. You think she wouldn't turn you in if it would show a profit?"

"I don't know the lady." Falconer lifted the hand with the cigar in it. "Ask yourself, or go back over the records: how many professional gamblers have ever been tied into narcotics or any of the other vice rackets?"

"I'll give you one right off the bat. El Guadalupe."

"Well, sure, but he was—as you very well know—a little off the norm about a lot of things."

"Remind me to write a treatise sometime," Smith said sourly. He brightened. "Anyway, you didn't deny knowing him, so we're making progress. Who gets the lay-out. Who're his heirs?"

"Is that what you were coming to see me about?"

"Yes."

"All right," Falconer nodded, "I'm damned if I don't tell you. Not that you couldn't find out anyway. He's got a mother and a sister somewhere down there. But the layout, except for his share, belongs to me."

"And you didn't know what he was doing," Smith said. He hummed a few bars of *Make Believe*. "The original innocent bystander, just a well-meaning country boy at heart."

For the first time Falconer's face showed emotion. His color deepened, the pleasant huskiness of his voice grew harsh with passion. "Listen, soldier, lay off me or I'll make you wish to Christ you had!"

"Excuse it," Smith said. Incredibly, the cop was still out there directing traffic around the gambler's car. Ordinary God-fearing citizens were being no end discommoded by Smith's. It seemed that this had been going on for an hour, though actually no more than five minutes had elapsed.

"Another thing," Falconer said. "If I were you I'd tell the monkeys you've got tailing me they aren't worth a damn. I could have lost them any time I felt like it."

"I'll mention it the first chance I get," Smith promised. "Meantime, you want something, I want something. There's a short cut that may get us both what we want. That's if you're leveling. If you're not, I'll be out more than you, but I'm a pretty fair gambler myself."

Falconer looked at his dead cigar with distaste, tossed it into the gutter. "I'm listening."

"There's a half-breed named Solano—Lupe's companion, lover, mistress—I never did know how these things work. I'd like to talk to him."

"All right, if I see him I'll tell him."

"That's not quite the same thing," Smith said. "I want you to fix it so he won't be trying to cut my throat while I'm talking."

"And what happens afterwards?"

Smith sighed. "He'll probably live to a ripe old age." His smile became amiable, even ingratiating. "You see, Georgie, you're in kind of a spot now. If he doesn't live, if anything unfortunate should happen to him in the very near future, you might easily be suspected of having arranged it."

There was a brief interval in which the night noises of a reasonably busy street seemed to swell and grow louder. Then Falconer said quietly: "I'll think it over, soldier. I may give you a ring later." He turned and nodded to Hefty. Together they went over and got into the limousine. Short-but-durable took the toothpick out of his mouth, looked at it, snapped it at the policeman's feet. Though his words were inaudible to Smith, there was that in his manner which suggested disparagement. He climbed leisurely under the wheel and the car rolled smoothly away.

Chapter 21

By La Jolla standards the house was a reasonably modest one, though even the town's very wealthy do not go in for spectacular architectural display. It was a single-storied, L-shaped house leaning slightly toward the *moderne* in the matter of picture windows and so on, set on a terraced corner lot offering a very fine view of curving coast line and of the million multicolored brilliants marking San Diego, ten or twelve miles distant. Two or three of the windows showed light behind discreetly drawn draperies. Occasional neighboring houses also showed light, as did the Van Owen mansion, which topped an adjacent knoll. It was a quiet, reserved street, withdrawn unto itself, dead-ending after three short blocks in a white-fenced cliff that dropped a hundred feet straight down to the ocean. There were no trees. It was not an ideal street in which to remain unobserved for any length of time. In a parked car half a block down from the house an operative named Fitzhugh complained to Smith that he felt positively naked.

"The cops have had a dozen phone calls about me," he said, "and the hell of it is, the citizens won't take no for an answer. A prowl car has got to come out to make sure it's still me, or Hansen, instead of a potential kidnapper, arsonist, or burglar. Then they report to the people who phoned, but it doesn't do any good." He sighed. "God help the thief who tries to make a living around here."

Smith thought this was very funny. "Where's Hansen now—under arrest?"

"Off chasing his particular pigeon some place," Fitzhugh said dispiritedly. "First his flies for a while, then mine. Then, just to vary the monotony, they both take a trip, but only to exercise their cars."

"They're wise to you?"

"My God, who wouldn't be!"

"I think maybe that's the Old Man's idea," Smith said. "Dynamite 'em." After a while he said: "I guess it's just as good as any other system, now. It loosened up Falconer—a little, anyway."

"I'll tell you one thing," Fitzhugh said. "These babies may not be the ones we're looking for, but they've been around. You can tell that by the way they lead you. And you know damned well they could shake you if they wanted to."

"Anybody can when he knows he's being tailed."

"Well, sure, but— You wouldn't by any chance be out here to relieve me, would you?"

"No, but you can go find yourself a tree if you want to. Which one's inside?"

"The duchess." Fitzhugh smacked his lips. "And if I weren't a married man—"

"When did that ever stop you?"

Fitzhugh was indignant. "You don't see my wife suing for a divorce, do you?"

"Why should she? She's probably out with three sailors right now."

Fitzhugh got out of his car and went off up the street. Presently a dog set up a terrific barking, and somebody turned his porch lights on. Fitzhugh came back wearing a harried expression and wiping his hands on his trousers. "Jesus Christ!" A black-and-white prowl car raced into the far end of the street. Its spotlight began combing shadowed lawns, clumps of shrubbery.

"Well, I'll see that you get plenty of cigarettes," Smith said. "I'll take care of your wife, too." He walked rapidly but quite openly down to the Lancaster house, mounted the steps, and rang the bell. The prowl car had halted beside Fitzhugh's when Eve Dudleigh opened the door.

She seemed only mildly surprised to see him. "Oh, it's Mr. Smith, isn't it?"

"All this and a memory too!" Smith marveled. He decided that she was just as vivid and exciting as he had remembered her. "Is your brother at home?"

"No," she said. "No, he isn't."

"Well, aren't you going to invite me in?"

"I don't know," she said, still with her hand on the doorknob. She was in black tonight, with touches of crimson at her throat and wrists. The crimson exactly matched her lipstick. In shadow her eyes were nearer blue than green. "I'm not sure that I like you, after all."

She stood aside. "I suppose you may as well come in." Briefly her gaze went past him to the street. "You've no car?"

"I left it around the corner," he said. "I didn't want to compromise you." He went into an oversize entrance hall. The house was bigger than it had appeared from outside. To the right was a living-room that must have been forty feet long. As he went toward it, carrying his hat, he discovered that she was not following and turned to see her standing with her back flat against the closed door. "Pardon me, you do live here, don't you?"

"Were you afraid of compromising my brother too?"

"Maybe." He contrived a small leer. "Though not exactly in the same way. You're expecting him back?"

"Of course. That is to say, I don't know how soon. Perhaps not even tonight." She abandoned her post by the door and came toward him. "I'm sorry if I seem to be inhospitable. You see, I've learned that you lied to me the other night—at least led me to believe you were something you're not."

He was indignant. "A fine thing! You did a little lying yourself."

"I?"

"About the burglar, remember? The one who didn't steal anything and you pretended to think it might be me? I suggested you report it to the police. You didn't. Deduction: there was no burglar."

Abruptly she laughed. "Rather elementary logic, and not without other possible interpretations." She crossed to stand in front of a mirror-framed fireplace which looked as though it had never been used. The logs of silver birch could have been hand-polished. "Would you care for a drink?"

"Yes," he said. "Yes, I would. As a matter of fact, you owe me one. Come to think of it, several."

Her smile was scornful. "Do you always demand payment in kind, Mr. Smith?"

He looked pointedly at her mouth. "Would you rather continued that other experiment?"

"I think not." She shook her head. "No, I'm quite sure not." She went out, returning presently with a tray on which were decanter and glasses. After she had poured, she said casually: "What did you want to see my brother about? Perhaps I can help you."

He sipped his drink, watching her. A curious revulsion of feeling came over him and he thought that this was a hell of a thing he was doing. With all the beauty in the world, all the loveliness, it seemed to be his lot to prove it something different. "I met a friend of his down in Los Gatos," he said carelessly. "Offhand, I'd say an old friend, though not in years." He smiled into her eyes. "Oddly enough, she reminded me of you. Younger, perhaps; not nearly so distinguished—indeed, a little common, I'm afraid—but really quite beautiful in her way." And as she half turned from him: "I'm not boring you?"

"No, I—not at all."

He admired her. His voice was tender. "You've such lovely eyes, precious. Are they like your mother's or your father's?"

"Father's, I think." The question only half roused her from some secret thought of her own. "Mother's were brown." She looked at him then, startled. "Why should that interest you?"

"I'm just showing off," he said. "You didn't think much of my deduction about the burglar. Here's one about your brother: he isn't your brother." As the glass slipped from her hand he moved nimbly, caught it before it crashed to the hearth. "Something known as the Mendelian Law," he said gently. "With one brown-eyed parent, the chance of both children having blue or green eyes is extremely remote."

Her face was pale, but composed. "And if this were true?"

"Throw him over," he urged. "Help me now, and when we nail him I'll do what I can to keep you out of it."

"This—this other woman: you're not just—"

"Making it up?" He shook his head. "I saw his picture on her dressing-table. She's here now, somewhere, with money and a hundred thousand dollars' worth of narcotics." He refilled her glass, forcibly curled her fingers around it. His face gave no indication of triumph; indeed, he felt none. "Do you think for one minute he's going to split with you?"

She drank mechanically, shivered a little. "Would you believe that I—knew nothing at all of this?"

His eyes glittered. "You were afraid of something when you first came to me. You're afraid of something now."

She nodded. "I thought it—you—all this new and extraordinary activity had to do with—" She looked at her empty glass, put it down carefully, as though its safety were very important to her. "At first it was to be just the usual shake-down, that's the way we planned it. Then, later, I got the idea I could marry him."

"Van Owen?"

"Yes." Again she shivered, though it was not cold in the room. Distantly surf broke against the cliff, swished on the beach. "You can make it difficult for me—I've a record of sorts, though I've never been convicted. As for Owen Van Owen, he'll be more hurt by this than by anything I've done to him up to now." She lifted her remarkable eyes to Smith's. "I'm really quite fond of him, you know."

He was suddenly and violently angry. "Listen, I don't give a damn about that. I want—"

"I know," she said quietly, "now." She stood up. "If I can help you, I will.

"Then help me."

But five minutes more got him nothing but background, which had to do with her own association with Lancaster. They had met in London, she said. She was not even sure that Lancaster was his right name. Once he had laughingly told her that he was officially dead; that the Japs were supposed to have got him in Hong Kong. Later, by way of Canada, they had come to the States and gradually worked their way west, trimming their suckers carefully and well and building up a stake against the time when the really big chance presented itself. Arrested on several occasions, they had bought their freedom by returning all or part of the money, or for lack of sufficient evidence. They were, she said —this without pride, indeed as though relating a somewhat distasteful fact—known as smooth workers.

All this she told him readily. But she steadfastly denied any knowledge of the narcotics angle. She either could not or would not clear up the thing that bothered him most, the thing that had prompted him to attempt, through Falconer, a contact with the half-breed Solano.

Dissatisfied, uneasy with the feeling that he should be somewhere else, that he was wasting his time expecting Lancaster to return here, he finally said good-night and drove back to town.

Chapter 22

As he entered his room the telephone began to ring. He went to it quickly. "Yes?"

The gray man's voice was mildly accusing. "You've been out to La Jolla."

"All right," he said angrily, "I've been out to La Jolla."

"The lady revealed something of interest?"

Smith scowled at his own reflection in a mirror opposite. "I don't know why I should tell you anything. You'll just twist it around to fit your own theories." He sighed. "All right, here's the crop." He repeated the information given him by Eve Dudleigh. "It looks straight enough, but I wouldn't try to sell it as gospel."

"Nor I," the gray man said. Then he said: "Her—ah—brother seems to have vanished. At least he's managed to give Hansen the slip."

"That's nice," Smith said with elaborate sarcasm. "That's about what one would expect, isn't it?" He yawned widely, audibly. "Well, don't bother me with your little troubles. Just go on master-minding and I'm sure everything will work itself out."

"What did George Falconer want?"

"Oh, so you know about that too!"

"Naturally. We're covering him, aren't we?"

"It's too bad you can't see me sneering," Smith said. "You've just lost one duck you were covering." He plucked at his lower lip for a moment. "Your guess is as good as mine. What he said he wanted was to be let alone. He's just an innocent gambler, et cetera, with only the public interest at heart."

"Do you believe that?"

"Good God!" Smith said furiously. "What do you care what I believe? I gave you the full deck, everything I had. Do you think I'm smarter than you are? Is that why you keep calling me up and sending guys like Cassidy around?" When there was nothing but silence at the other end he said more mildly: "I gave Falconer a little test. He hasn't turned in the answers yet."

"Nothing you care to tell me about?"

"No," Smith said, adding nastily that it wasn't because he wanted to be a boy hero, either. "Under your astute management this case has got leakier than a busted sieve. This is one item that the fewer people know about it, the better. I'm beginning to think that even two is too many."

"Well, perhaps you're right," the gray man said. He disconnected gently. Smith cradled his own instrument and sat there on an arm of the chesterfield, looking at nothing in particular.

The telephone rang. He snatched it up. "Yes?" Then he said incredulously: "Who?"

It was Juanita Regan.

"Darling," she said, speaking very rapidly, "I know you must hate me, and with reason too, but I'm trying to make it up to you now. Will you promise me something if I help you, if I tell you what you want to know?"

For a moment Smith's image in the mirror almost frightened him. He looked thoroughly depraved. "What do I want to know?"

"Who the big wheel is. Who's got the stuff."

Quite suddenly he began to laugh. He shook with laughter. "You mean you've finally met someone trickier than you are? I don't believe it."

She cursed him. She cursed viciously and at length someone she carefully avoided naming. Then she said breathlessly: "Listen, I'm not asking for money. Now that I know who you are I can't expect that. All I want is protection and—and immunity for anything you've got against me. That isn't so very much to ask, is it? It isn't as if you weren't a dick and out to cop me if you could. What I did to you was only—And anyway, I'm making it up to you now, aren't I?"

"You didn't know I was a dick at the time," he pointed out. "I was a guy helping you. Like the kid you seduced and tricked and made a louse out of." He drew an angry breath. "Make your deal with the cops, baby."

"No, I— Please, Smith, I'm scared. I need someone I can trust." Something like a puppy's whimper came over the wire. "I tell you I'm scared, scared, scared! Can't you understand that?"

"Of what?"

Her teeth were definitely chattering now. "There's only one thing for a girl like me to be afraid of. Will you—?" Again there was the small, puppy-like sound.

"Why don't you just tell me this guy's name and let me

take care of him from here?" Smith asked reasonably. "You're not to scared to be awfully damned coy about that."

"No, I've no means of knowing how many others he's— You wouldn't come if I told you now. Something might happen, all kinds of things could happen, so that even— Listen, if I tell you where I am you've got to promise me that no one else will know. Not anybody, understand?"

"All right, we'll skip the big one for a moment." He held his right hand out at arm's length, watching it for some sign of trembling. It was quite steady. "How about a little something on account, just a sample to show you're halfway on the level?"

"Would I be calling you if I— My God, what have you got to lose?" When he did not answer she cursed him for a cautious old woman, and herself for ever thinking he was anything else. She ran out of breath. Then, the words running over themselves in her haste to get them out, she described and named the masters of two ships; she named the ships and their registry, one Dutch, the other Panamanian. She described the boat she had used to get out to the larger vessels, a speedster she said was hidden in the marshes north of Los Gatos. "El Guadalupe found out about my racket and hitched his onto it. Now are you satisfied?"

"It'll have to do, I suppose."

"And you'll promise what I asked you?"

He licked his lips. His eyes were jet-hard, bright, and unwinking. "About coming alone, yes."

"But you'll do what you can about the other?"

"Yes."

"Then listen." She gave him an address over in East San Diego. "Apartment 7." She managed a shaky laugh. "For luck."

"What's the phone number?"

"My God," she wailed, "there isn't any! I'm in a booth down on the corner and every second I stand here is—"

"Read me that one, then." Presently he said: "All right, fifteen minutes, twenty at the most;" and with a finger broke the connection. Instantly opening the circuit he asked the girl on the switchboard downstairs to see what she could do with a supervisor about fitting the phone number to a street address. Waiting, he frowned at a dull smear on the otherwise polished tip of one shoe. He rubbed it on a trouser leg. When the operator came back on the line he said: "Yes?" and presently: "Thank you."

Juanita Regan had been telling the truth about one thing, anyway.

His face once more placid, whistling a trifle absently between his teeth, he got a gun from a dresser drawer, put it in his topcoat pocket, put on his hat, turned out the lights, and went back down to the hotel garage.

Driving swiftly across town, he used only moderate precautions to see that he was not followed. It was a comparatively slack hour in traffic, not yet eleven, and neither the theaters nor bars had emptied their crowds into the streets. He thought, a very little, about what he was going to do if this happened, or if such-and-such happened, but thinking of that sort was never any good. Things never turned out the way you expected them, not even if you gave them three alternatives. And outguessing Juanita was like trying to grasp a handful of quicksilver. He thought it not unlikely that since she had confessed to him—indeed, boasted of the killing of Guadalupe—she might now be intent on rectifying that error by killing him too. He rather hoped that were so. It would make his own job of work a bit more pleasurable.

When he came into the street he sought, he saw that it was a minor business artery, though all the stores except a confectionery next a neighborhood movie house were closed. A few cars were parked along the curbs, not many. A half dozen or so passed him in the next three blocks. When he found the address, it was on the glass door of a narrow entrance hall between two store fronts. Dimly lighted stairs led upward to flats or apartments above the row of stores. The apartments boasted no name, merely the street numerals. The hallway was clean, untenanted. He drove on past to the corner, where a closed Standard Oil station had only its small night light burning. A public telephone booth stood isolated from the main building, accessible to the sidewalk.

He drove on around the block, seeing no one who appeared interested in either him or the apartment building. Then, quickly, he ran the car into the paved area surrounding the service station, where he would have less chance of being blocked than if he parked at the curb. On foot he went back to the narrow entrance, looked once up and down the street, went in. There was a row of ten glass-fronted mail boxes set into the imitation marble wall at the foot of the stairs. Apartment 7's box was labeled in smudged handwriting: "Brody."

He went up the stairs two at a time, swiftly but without noise. He heard no sound until he came to the top, where behind one of the closed doors someone was fiddling with a radio, which alternately blasted and mumbled. Evidently the guy was an addict of crime programs; a rash of pistol shots broke out from time to time. Smith moved along the hall quietly, but without stealth. When he faced Number 7 he knocked, not loudly, but not furtively either, and stood quickly back to one side, out of line with the door.

There was no answer.

He counted ten, holding his breath. Then, flattening himself against the wall beside the door, he put his right hand in his topcoat pocket. His left darted out to seize the doorknob, twist it. He flung the door inward. No one did anything about it. There was no sound, nothing at all. Then very faintly to his nostrils came the unmistakable smell of recently burned cordite. He knew with almost utter certainty what he would find when he went into the room.

He found it.

She was lying half on, half off the let-down wall bed. She still had on her street coat, and a dark scarf tied under her chin, peasant-fashion, hid most of her dark red curls. For a moment he thought that she was still breathing, but she wasn't. Even as he looked at her the lovely, violet-shaded eyes opened and stayed open. There were two scorched holes in the breast of her tweed coat. Blood was only now beginning to well from them. Beneath her trailing right hand, on the cheap axminster carpet, lay a gun. Something about one of the worn butt-plates set his nerves to jumping crazily. He bent and with a handkerchief picked the weapon up. It was his. It was the one for which she had substituted Cassidy's, which in turn she had got from her father and used on Guadalupe.

Twice she had framed him. Even dying, she had framed him. A kind of panic seized him then. Laughter like hiccups issued from drawn-back lips; his face was yellow. Still holding the gun, he forced himself to look at the apartment, objectively, inch by inch. Except for an open suitcase and the let-down bed there was no sign that the place was lived in, had ever been lived in. He became aware of a siren rising to a crescendo very close at hand. He ran out, considered briefly looking for back stairs, decided against it; the front were nearer him, nearer to his car. He ran down them. Beyond the glass of the front door a uniformed policeman went by, running. Smith went out, turning in the opposite direction. Captain Dietrich came around the corner from the Standard Oil lot, saw him. His gun was already out and he halted, spread-legged, balanced to shoot, eager for the slightest provocation. "Drop that rod, Smith."

Behind Smith there was the larruping pound of flat feet, the copper coming back. Smith dropped the gun. With the handkerchief he wiped his sweating palms, moved toward Dietrich. "You do get around," he said. "I was just about to call you."

"Yeah, I'll bet."

Smith fell down in the path of the running patrolman. The man's body plunged over him, hit Dietrich, knocked him sprawling. Dietrich's gun went off, and somewhere a window shattered, showering glass on cement. On his feet again, Smith skidded around the corner to see Dietrich's car directly behind his own. The door was open, the motor running. He took it. With the siren wide open he ran it the hell away from there.

Behind him there was a lot of yelling, a lot of shooting. Nothing came of it.

Chapter 23

It was the kind of flophouse where no questions are asked so long as you pay your dollar; where the manager, when he answers the tap bell on the battered counter under the scrofulous mail- and key-rack, does not look at you, so that in case he is asked later he can say truthfully that he doesn't remember. It was the kind of place patronized by the sediment of society: cheap touts and hustlers and petty crooks and poolroom habitués; the kind of place where cops might borrow a room in which to question a suspect a little more thoroughly than they could at headquarters.

Narrow stairs whose worn rubber treads smelled strongly of disinfectant led upward from a street noisy with streetcars, taxis, juke boxes. At the head of the stairs, beside the "office," Smith replaced the receiver on the wall phone and stood for a moment considering one more call. He was in his shirt sleeves, his collar open, his tie loosened. Other odors than the disinfectant twitched at his nostrils: frying hot dogs, chili, beer, sour wine. He wished he had a hot dog, one with chili on it, though he knew it would not be good for his ulcers, imaginary or otherwise. A prowl car went by, its siren screaming. He decided against making the other call and returned to his room halfway down the long hall. From behind some of the doors he passed there came sounds of occupancy, but they were vague sounds, almost furtive.

The room had an old-fashioned once-white iron bed, an oak dresser, two straight chairs, a scarred linoleum rug. The one window gave on a narrow shaft beyond which was a blank brick wall. In one corner was a small square sink, its porcelain etched by rust from a leaky faucet. On hooks screwed into dun-colored plaster his topcoat, suit coat, and hat looked curiously out of place. They should have been shabbier or louder. He decided that it did not matter, since they could not be seen from the hall.

He opened the transom above the door about a third of the way. He got his gun and a recently purchased newspaper from his topcoat pockets, placed one of the chairs carefully against the wall abutting the hall, and sat on it. His face was expectant but not worried.

From time to time feet came up the stairs, paused briefly while their owner got a key from the rack, came on down past his door or went in the other direction. His ears became attuned to each new sound in the hall, even though the rumble and crash of a bowling alley echoed in the shaft beyond his window. Once he got up and adjusted the blind on this, not because it was possible for anyone to see in, but because the glass reflected part of the room. He returned to his chair and his listening.

It was ten minutes past midnight when a newcomer paused at the battered counter just a little longer than was necessary to pick up a key. Smith imagined he could hear the dog-eared register being opened, pages being turned, but he knew that this was impossible. His mind might be hearing it, his ears weren't. Then he realized that there was no longer any sound at all from the hall, nothing. He stood up, flat against the wall, only his head turned toward the door. He rustled the newspaper. With his mouth tight shut he cleared his throat. He rustled the newspaper again.

The doorknob turned slowly, very gently, under an experimental hand. It kept on turning till the latch was fully released. The door moved inward perhaps an eighth of an inch. Then it opened and Captain Dietrich came in with it.

Putting everything he had into the blow, Smith chopped down on Dietrich's gun wrist. Bone snapped under the impact. Dietrich's gun fell and went skittering across the floor. Then the two men were locked in a furious, but uneven and short-lived struggle. No matter how willing its owner, how pain-maddened and kill-crazy, a broken arm is a terrific handicap. Especially the right one, the strong one. Smith dropped him.

The door had banged shut sometime during the battle, and he stood there leaning against it, breathing gustily, listening. They must have made considerable noise, but apparently no one was going to investigate it. This was a far cry from places like La Jolla: the neighbors, though possibly curious, were not snoopy. He felt that he had made an excellent choice.

He had not come off entirely unscathed, for Dietrich, even with one arm out of commission, was still quite a man. A sleeve hung in ribbons; blood ran down his jaw and neck from three deep slashes on one cheek; his intestines had knots tied in them as a result of a knee in the wrong place.

Presently Dietrich stirred a little. His eyes came half-open, closed again, suddenly opened very wide. "Where—uh—? How did—?" Recognition hit him, and memory, and as he tried to use his right arm, pain. "You son of a bitch!"

"There's always that," Smith said. He went over to the basin, drew a glass of water. "Drink?"

"Yeah."

Smith brought it to him. Dietrich seized the wrist above the glass, dragged Smith down on top of him. They flailed each other around for a minute, but again it couldn't last. When the older, stockier man finally lay quiscent he was not out, just thoroughly exhausted.

Smith said, panting a little: "You might as well make up your mind to it, Floyd."

"Maybe. Some of the boys will be along presently."

"Not the way you came," Smith said. "This time you played it alone. You're going to stay alone, except for me, until I'm done with you. He went to his coat, got out cigarettes, matches. "Smoke?"

"Yeah."

Smith lit one for himself, another from that, and tossed the second across to the man on the floor. He read disappointment in Dietrich's eyes. "You're a tricky bastard, Floyd. There's none trickier, nor crookeder, than a crooked cop." He laughed smoke out of his mouth. "What'd you do to Regan to get her all riled up—tell her to shove off, it was your dough in the first place?"

Dietrich burned half an inch of cigarette before he said: "I don't mind telling you. You say I'm alone here. Well,

I happen to know that you're alone too. So we'll know what we know, and when I go out of here in a little while, as I most surely will, it'll be all forgotten."

Smith's eyes sharpened a trifle. Otherwise his face gave no indication that he was more than politely interested. Dietrich watched him for a moment, saying nothing. Then he asked if he might sit in a chair. "This arm is kind of giving me hell."

"Try the bed," Smith suggested. He watched Dietrich get slowly to his knees and one good hand. He watched the man's muscles tense, the head come up ever so little, ready for a line plunge at the goal, which in this case was the pistol lying over against the baseboard. He took one long step and booted Dietrich's left rump, toppling him over. Then he picked up the pistol. "Keep trying, Floyd. Slug it out to the finish." His face was suddenly hard, cruel. "They teach you that in police school, don't they?"

"Yes," Dietrich said. He got to his feet, stood there in his familiar spread-legged stance. "But like you say, a bad cop learns other things as he goes along. They learn to protect themselves in the clinches if it's anyways possible." His own face grew cruel, his eyes bright with malice. "I didn't know how much the redhead might have told you over the phone. Unfortunately, when I taxed her with it, she flourished a gun and it kind of went off. Unfortunately too, I didn't get to shoot you as I'd planned. That left me with but one thing to do. I did it. Have you any idea what it is was I did?"

"Yes," Smith said.

" 'Twas my thought that we could make a deal. The lady in exchange for your forgetfulness?"

"No," Smith said.

"For a free running start, then?"

Smith's face was pale, sweat made it shiny, unhealthy-looking. "No." He swallowed with some difficulty. "For anything else I might do it. Maybe I might do it. But yours is a nasty racket. It's nasty for anybody, but for a cop—" He looked down at Dietrich's gun in his hand, licked his lips. "You're going to tell me what I want to know, Floyd. I'm going to work on you until you do."

Dietrich shook his head. "You can maybe make me go in with you, or you can carry me in. With what there is showing, it's doubtful which of us takes the big rap. But the other I don't think you can do."

"You don't know me very well," Smith said. His pallor

deepened; his eyes glittered. "Nobody does." He put his face down close to Dietrich's. "Would you like to try praying, Floyd? Or yelling?" He laughed and twisted sidewise as Dietrich's knee came up; he wrested his gun arm free of Dietrich's grip. The gun rose, fell. Dietrich dropped senseless to the floor. "Sporting, you know," Smith said to no one.

He went over and closed the transom, jammed a chairback under the doorknob. Returning to the bed he jerked a sheet from it, methodically tore it into strips. Not without effort he lifted Dietrich to the bed, lashed his ankles and good arm to corner posts. He could not bring himself to touch the broken arm. From another strip he fashioned a gag, but did not attempt to put it on. He went over to the basin in the corner, where he drank two glasses of water. A third glassful, the second chair, and the newspaper he carried back to the bedside.

He sat on the chair, spread the newspaper on his knees. Ejecting the cartridges from Dietrich's gun, he put his pocket knife to work on them, loosening the lead, removing it, dumping the cordite from shell to paper. He had quite a little pile of it when he saw Dietrich's eyes watching him.

"What's that for?"

He did not answer.

Dietrich filled his lungs with air.

Smith stoppered the open mouth with a fist. Without spilling a grain of the powder he transferred the newspaper from his knees to the bed. He showed Dietrich the gag. "I'll use this if I have to," he said. "If I do, I may not be able to tell when you've had enough."

Dietrich let his pent-up breath out through his nose.

With his free hand Smith unbuttoned Dietrich's vest, unbuckled the shoulder harness. He hooked his fingers in Dietrich's collar, ripped collar, tie, shirt, and undershirt down to the belt. He lumped the cordite on Dietrich's naked belly, at the navel.

"This stuff burns like hell," he said in a conversational tone. "They tried it out on me down in Nogales once. Took the skin-grafters six months to get a fix on it." He struck a match.

Sweat stood out on Dietrich's forehead in oily globules. For a long moment his eyes stared incredulously into Smith's. Then he groaned.

Smith took his fist away from Dietrich's mouth. The match burned itself out.

"I believe you'd do it," Dietrich said hoarsely.

"I would," Smith said. "I will."

Dietrich sighed. "I guess I'm getting too old for this sort of thing now," he said.

Chapter 24

In a comparatively quiet room at police headquarters the gray man and Acting Chief Martin Gahagan faced each other across the chief's broad desk. The chief himself was at a convention in Atlantic City, which may have been a fortunate thing. In a tight little group, watching them, were Linda, Cassidy and Smith. At a table against a side wall a plain-clothes sergeant and a civil clerk were sorting out Captain Dietrich's effects, papers, records, and so on taken from him, from his car, his home. Much of it had already been gone over, but they were checking it again. Dietrich himself was in the jail hospital, and they had not yet asked him to sign a confession, since there was no hurry about it, considering Linda and the evidence already collected.

"This is bad business," Gahagan said. He was a heavy-faced, white-haired man with the indelible look of a cop grown old in the service. He was pretty thoroughly cut up over Dietrich. "A very bad business."

"It is," the gray man agreed. "I have recently had a similar experience myself, though the lad was not strictly a member of my staff."

Under his breath Smith said: "The hypocritical old son of a bitch. In a day or two he won't admit ever having heard Bittner's name."

Linda looked at him. "Mustn't be nasty, darling." She made her eyes big. "My hero!" She seemed absolutely unruffled by her experience, though she could easily have starved to death in the spot Dietrich had hidden her.

"There are things I do not yet understand," Gahagan said. His eyes, meeting Smith's, were curiously apologetic. "How did you tag him in the first place?"

"He damned near killed me," Smith said. "He wanted to. I saw him wanting to." He described the street scene out in East San Diego. "That made him popping up at the opportune moment just once too often for it to be coincidence. I remembered the shooting of the punk, Ralph, which at the time seemed nothing more than a too enthusiastic cop knocking off a cop-killer. Looking back, I'd had him in my hair at other times he might have thought critical: right after I'd talked to Falconer, and again when I got back from Los Gatos. His excuses were not illogical, but I saw now that he was afraid I'd learned something dangerous to him personally."

He put his hard stare on Linda. "Remember what happened when I was putting you in your car this evening?"

Her voice was almost inaudible. "Yes."

"Remember what I'd told you a little while before that?"

She nodded.

"So he guessed that maybe you meant something to me," he said. His face was coldly furious. "It gave him a whip over me, and I don't like that kind of pressure. I don't like myself when I have to fight it." He began pacing the room. In a thick, unnatural voice he described in minute detail what had occurred in the flophouse bedroom.

When he had finished, all the color had drained from Linda's face. Her eyes held a kind of horror. "Suppose he— Would you have—?"

For a moment it was as though there was no one else in the room. They stared at each other. Then he laughed harshly. "What do you think?"

She moistened her lips. "Because of me?"

He decided he had gone a trifle too far. He wanted her to be thoroughly sick of him. He did not want her wrestling with a guilt complex the rest of her life. "Don't let it go to your head," he said carelessly. "That was only part of it."

Cassidy, with a gentleness utterly foreign to him, touched her shoulder. "Don't let him get you down, baby." He brightened. "I don't know what you ever saw in the guy, anyway. Now take a man like me, you could practically twist him around your little finger."

She gave him a small, appreciative smile. "Is that offer still open for wiener schnitzel and a short beer?"

"Any time of the day or night."

"I'm going to take you up on it presently," she said. Then, her composure completely restored: "Do go on, Mr. Smith. We are all so interested in your adventures."

Smith lit a cigarette, addressed himself to Gahagan. "Sorry I got off on the wrong foot there. It's not too easy, now, to separate what he did and how I knew he had done it."

Gahagan said evenly, pleasantly: "Tell it in your own way, then, only minding that we know the ins and outs of it."

Smith thought for a moment. "This was still second-guessing, you understand, but I remembered her fright when she phoned me; the Regan girl, I'm talking about. I could see now, or thought I could, that it was because I'd suggested she go to the police. She'd had her experience with one cop. She didn't know how many, or which ones, were outside his sphere of influence."

Gahagan sighed heavily. There was genuine sorrow in his tone. " 'Tis a sad fact that in the public mind a bad cop is like the apple in the barrel." His eyes sharpened. "Her experience, you say?"

Smith nodded. "She'd killed one man, Guadalupe, because she didn't think he was giving her enough. She'd gone to a lot of trouble and used considerable ingenuity delivering a load for which she expected a hundred thousand dollars. Dietrich gave her a thousand and told her to go roll a hoop." He crushed out his cigarette in a tray on the desk. "From Dietrich's point of view he was being generous. His money financed the original purchase. He had already lost a twenty-grand shipment to us. And literally her greed was responsible for smearing the entire Mexican set-up." He drew a deep breath, remembering his part in that. "Well, she was just not the kind you could do that to. After a couple of sessions with her, Dietrich himself realized it. He was on his way to fix her wagon when he saw her leaving the phone booth."

"So he killed her?"

"He killed her. Not exactly in the way he intended, nor did he know it was my gun she flashed on him. That would have been a break for him—it certainly was a bad one for me—if things had worked out differently."

The gray man prodded him gently. "The patrolman?"

"Made it look authentic," Smith said. "A nice touch. Dietrich had no means of knowing how much she had told me over the phone. He wasn't even sure it was me she called. But he was damned sure she was expecting someone, so he waited around outside till I showed. He knew then he was going to have to kill me. He simply hustled up the beat cop, pointed out my car, and told him she must be in the neighborhood too. Then he sent the bull barging down the street and waited for me."

From under beetling white brows Gahagan stared at the gray man. "Well, I suppose the whole thing will have to come out."

"He's going up," Gregg said. "Make no mistake about that. My division can do it, or the FBI can nail him with the kidnap charge." He drew reflectively on his cigar, blew aromatic smoke at the ceiling. "We don't have to make a nation-wide scandal of it."

Gahagan appeared to find some small comfort in that. "And the two killings?"

"They'd be tricky things to prosecute." He continued to regard the ceiling. "I've an idea my man Smith knew that, which is why he had to—ah—do what he did."

Smith said furiously to Cassidy: "His man Smith!"

"That's the executive type for you."

Smith did not look at Linda; his whole attention appeared to be on Cassidy's face. "What did Lancaster have to say when you finally found him?"

"He said he just got tired not being able to go to the whatsit without a dick nudging him." Cassidy laughed. "And that picture you thought was so important: he said it must have been taken seven-eight years ago when they were teamed up for a while in China. Trouble came, she was evacuated, he wasn't." He laughed again. "She must've been mourning his memory." He leaned forward to peer with mock anxiety into Smith's eyes. "Have I hurt you, lover boy?"

"Not about that. It's just your clumsy efforts to queer me with Miss Van Owen, here."

"Christ, after the exhibition you put on out there in the middle of the floor I don't have to do a thing, just sit tight." He leered at Linda. "Right?"

"Right."

Cassidy's eyes suddenly got a worried look. Again he peered into Smith's face. He said angrily: "I didn't tell you a damned thing, did I?"

"Sure you did. You told me what Lancaster said."

"But before that," Cassidy insisted. "You held out on us. You knew something we didn't."

"No," Smith said. "I just wondered about something you didn't." His face was placid, amiable. "I wondered why Miss Regan would have to pull out Lupe's fingernails, trying to learn the identity of someone she already knew."

Cassidy's voice was choked with rage. He appealed to Linda. "You see how tricky he is? There's just no trusting the bastard."

"I know," she said sympathetically. The golden glints were once more back in her eyes. "I'll always be grateful to you for exposing him."

Smith looked at her briefly, looked away. "You should have gone home with your father."

"My father was in a very great hurry to find someone else."

"He could do worse. She's quite a woman."

"She is," Linda agreed.

"There was a time you didn't think so."

"That was before I started chasing a detective." She corrected that to: "A brutal detective."

Cassidy stood up, yawning widely. "Have fun, people. You bore me." Halfway across to the conference at the other side of the room, he turned and came back. "Tell me, master mind: how'd you sucker Dietrich into coming after you?"

Smith affected a becoming modesty. "Aw, it was nothing, really." Then he said angrily: "I kept thinking about that bitch and her reaction when Lupe died without talking. She didn't know who his contact in the States was. The next time I saw her she did know. It seemed reasonable that she might have got the information from Solano. I tried to find Solano. I couldn't. I got Falconer to find him, but he wouldn't talk to me, not even through Falconer." He became angrier. "He still thinks I knocked off his queen, damn it. He's probably gunning for me right now."

Cassidy thought this was very funny. He laughed uproariously. He laughed so hard that he broke up the conference. The gray man and Captain Gahagan came over. "A good laugh wouldn't hurt any of us," Gahagan said. He looked from one to another of their faces. "Or is it a secret, now?"

Cassidy told him, enjoying every word of it. Abruptly he realized that Smith had not yet answered his question. His face became congested. "All right, come on," he snarled. "Let's see the rabbit!"

Smith stared at nothing at all for a moment, his eyes curiously blank, without luster. Then he said: "He didn't know it was me putting the bite on him. He thought it was Solano trying for a cut and naturally he wasn't going to stand for it." His eyes came alive, were filled with sudden fury as they met the gray man's. "It was my terrific Spanish accent that fooled him. You were so right!" He turned and stalked out.

In the corridor Linda caught up with him, put her body between his and the exit. They studied each other with mutual dislike. Then with a little cry she threw herself into his arms. "Oh, darling, darling, Cassidy is right, you know. You're such a bastard!"

"I know," he said in a discouraged voice.

Standing on tiptoe, she put her mouth on his, fiercely. He pushed her away. "I just thought of something," he said. "Did you ever try kissing with your eyes open?"

"Of course, silly!"

"You did?" He stared at her. "Well, it's certainly damned funny I've never noticed it before."

Her sigh was one of exasperation. "There must be a moral in this, somewhere," she said. "You would have if your own hadn't been closed."

TO THE READER

If you enjoyed this book, you will be glad to know that there are many others just as well written, just as interesting, to be had in the Fiction House Press Library.

You will find the Fiction House Press Library online at

www.FictionHousePress.com

www.ingramcontent.com/pod-product-compliance
Lightning Source LLC
LaVergne TN
LVHW091000080826
845145LV00003B/1075